BIG (99 DADDIES BOOK 2)

CASEY COX

ISBN: 978-0-6489983-3-4

www.caseycoxbooks.com

This book is a work of fiction. It is not your weekly grocery shopping list. Have a look under your kitchen table, it might have slipped under there. Any references to real people, organizations, bubble gum flavors, restaurants, baked goods, locations and TV shows are simply intended to offer a semblance of reality and are completely fictitious. Characters, names, plot points and dialogue are figments of the author's imagination...and the result of caffeine overstimulation.

I would like to say a special thank you to my amazing Beta team for their overall amazingness, insightful suggestions and brilliant advice: Rachael, Brady, Tammy, Jill, Alyson and LJ. Thank you x infinity!

SYNOPSIS

Big: (adjective)
Large, as in size, height, width, or amount.
See also: Nick "Big Boy Energy" Macklin.

A Daddy who has everything money can buy...
Except the one boy he can't have.

You've never met a boy like Nick Macklin. He's an enigma, wrapped in warm cinnamon pastry, wearing a belly-exposing tank top. He's two hundred and forty pounds of confident, cocky, curvy yumminess.

He's proud of his body and proud to be a big boy. He's also loud, unfiltered, loyal, and fiercely independent. In other words, everything smart, successful, sexy silver fox Daddy Steel Crawford has ever wanted in a boy.

There's just one problem: Nick thinks Steel's a jerk.

One of those guys that can get what he wants, simply because he's a man with the means to afford it. Steel might be a self-made man, and able to catch Nick's eye—but that doesn't guarantee he'll automatically be able to capture Nick's heart.

Even if he is a super successful lawyer who runs his own law firm. Even if he is as kind as he is rich, and a genuinely decent guy. Even if his light blue eyes, silver mane, and sculpted body have earned him the title of one of Daylesford's Most Eligible Daddies—three years running.

Steel is a Daddy who can buy anything he wants, but will Nick be the one thing he can't have?

BIG
Big is a Daddy-lite enemies-to-lovers gay romance featuring a one-in-a-million big boy being pursued by a sexy silver fox Daddy.

Come along for the ride and enjoy some crazy/sexy/cool shenanigans including: sexy go-go dancers, erotic cake-sitting, a scene-by-scene recreation of an iconic '90s flashmob, plenty of zingy one-liners, a crew of sassy friends, lots of LOLs, and all the feels on the way to a heartwarming HEA.

Big is the second book in the *99 Daddies* series. Each book in the series will contain overlapping characters and storylines, so you may enjoy them more by reading them in order.

99 DADDIES
99 Daddies is a hilarious, entertaining, and heartwarming contemporary/new adult Daddy-lite MM romance series.

Escape to Daylesford, the (fictional) Daddy capital of America. If you love steamy and complex Daddy/boy dynamics, May-

December gay romances with a twist, sweet and sassy MM age gap romances—and chasing those guaranteed HEAs—you'll love it here.

So come along and meet the 99 Daddies of Daylesford. Who will be YOUR favorite?

CHAPTER ONE

NICK

If my life were a movie, this would be the opening sequence where I'm walking down the street in slow motion looking deffers fab-u-lous with some retro cute '80s tune playing in the background. You know, something about walking on sunshine or some other crazy '80s shit.

The sun actually was shining down brightly, beautifully lighting up my bouncy, shoulder-length, chocolate-brown hair, and bringing out the bling of the diamond-encrusted *sASSy* emblazoned across my black tank top.

Sassy. Not just a tank top logo, but a word that described me perfectly.

I'd be played by one of the Chrises—Pratt, Pine, Hemsworth, or Evans—the exact one doesn't really matter. I'm sure any one of them would be able to capture my complex nuances just fine, as well as my insane ability to blow big-ass bubbles with gum, which, frankly, is a criminally underappreciated skill.

But whichever one of them it was, they'd definitely need to go on a special diet for the part. None of that *chicken and rice six times a day followed by two hours at the gym* bullshit. No, to play a big boy like me, they'd have to look the part, too.

I love my body. I love my size. All two hundred and forty pounds. Always have. It's me, after all, so why wouldn't I?

I was, as my grandma would say, a big-boned child. I guess that was her way of calling me big without making me feel bad about it. That's why I call myself big now. It's my way of reclaiming a word that has been used against me, like a weapon, for pretty much my entire life.

Being a plus-size boy at school was about as much fun as it sounds. Being a plus-size *gay* boy at school was just the dairy-free icing on the low-fat, gluten-free, sugar-free cake. I learned pretty early on that there was nowhere for me to hide, as in literally, because I just couldn't fit in anywhere. Hide and seek was still a trigger for me as an adult. *I kid, I kid.*

My size actually became my superpower. I figured if I can't hide, and everyone had an opinion about my body—which they were more than happy to share with me—then I would turn it on its head. I would make this work for me. No, scratch that—I would own the fuck out of it.

Yes, I'm a big boy. I've got quads and biceps that bulge with muscles as hard as a rock, a soft, round and slightly hairy belly, and an ass that any of the Kardashians would pay good money for. And yes, I'm gay, like *rainbows, unicorns, and midriff-baring tank tops as my normal everyday outfit* gay.

Sure, sometimes people have a problem with me. I'm too loud. Too opinionated. Too out there. Just *too much.* And that's fine. If people have something to say to me, I'd be happy to meet them and take their complaints at the corner of Eighth Street and GoFuckYourself Avenue.

Because even if I could, I refuse to hide who I am. Period.

So yeah, the casting agent for my inevitable biopic would need to take that into consideration.

I've also always been a damn hard worker. This big boy casually sauntering down the street was juggling four jobs. I worked as a naked butler with my best friend Mikey (*But you already knew that, didn't you?* the voiceover would say as I'd turn to the camera for a cheeky wink). I was a dancer at The Tank Top, Daylesford's best go-go bar. I worked as a clown-slash-magician at children's parties, and I helped my grandparents out with their bakery.

Seeing as they raised me, there was no way I wasn't going to do everything I could to support them, especially as they were fighting with a greedy developer who wanted to demolish their bakery. The bakery that they'd owned for over forty-five years. That's, like, since before Madonna became a thing. There was no way in hell I was going to sit back and let that happen.

Which brings me to the beginning of my story, and explains why I was walking down one of Daylesford's busiest downtown streets, carrying a seven-layer tiered cake. The cake was one of the latest creations from my grandparents' bakery.

I had taken a quick peek at it when I picked it up and it looked amazing, decorated beautifully in alternating tiers of deep blue and sparkling white, just like the client wanted. I only wished grandma didn't spend so much time on baking the actual cakes themselves. It wasn't about the taste, no one ever actually ate them. But how could I explain that to her?

As I looked up, the neon lights of The Tank Top sign reflected in my five-dollar yellow gas station sunglasses. Cue the part in the movie where they played my backstory montage. You know the bit with the wide-eyed and innocent country boy getting off the Greyhound, happy he'd finally made it to the big city, but also scared because he'd never travelled more than twenty miles outside of Bumfuck, USA.

Except I'd lived in Daylesford all of my life and there was no way in hell you'd ever catch me on a Greyhound. Those things didn't even have business class.

Besides, my backstory wasn't really all that sad. Sure, I was raised by my grandparents because I had a deadbeat dad who disappeared before I was even born and a flighty mother who was in and out of my life almost as much as she was in and out of rehab.

But Grandma and Gramps more than made up for my crappy parents. They were literally the best and gave me a wonderful childhood. It wasn't possible to have been showered with any more love and affection than what they gave me.

I reached the front door of The Tank Top and silently prayed that Tristan, the bar manager, had remembered to leave it unlocked for me. It was mid-afternoon, so the bar wasn't open yet. I gave the door a gentle nudge and thankfully, it opened with its usual loud creak. I'd been holding the cake the entire seven blocks from the bakery to the bar, so it was starting to get heavy. I walked in and placed the cake at the edge of the bar.

As I walked back to lock the front door, I yelled out, "Hey, Tristan, I'm here."

I gave the door a firm push and secured the deadbolt. When I returned to the bar, I saw Tristan and our newest go-go boy, Sam.

"Is that the cake?" Tristan asked.

I didn't even bother to hide my laughter.

"No, Einstein," I said. "I just like walking around Daylesford with an empty cake box."

"Smartass," he said as his lips tugged upward. "I've just never seen a cake that's going to be used for...whatever the hell it is you're going to use it for."

"What—what are you going to be using it for?" Sam asked, a little nervously.

He'd only joined us two weeks earlier and was still finding his feet. He actually *was* from Bumfuck, USA, so this was the *leaving a small town to make it in the big city* part of his life.

His reddish hair, wide blue eyes, and freckled nose totally fit into the small-town country-boy vibe. The jaw-dropping, hip-twisting, gyrating moves he'd whip out on the podium, did not. Hmm, he'd be a tough one to cast.

Whereas Sam was a newbie boy, Tristan was the Daddy of the go-go boys. He was pushing thirty-five and way more of a man than a boy. Broad shoulders, a thick hairy chest, legs that went on for days. In fact, he was the exact opposite of a boy, and you can bet your bottom dollar the Daddy-chaser clients ate him up.

The Tank Top had twelve go-go dancers and we were the best go-go bar in town. The competition, if you could call it that, came from two other bars. The Blade used to be good, until they changed owners about a year ago and the service went downhill. D.I.C.K (Daddy Issues Come Knocking) had a cool name, but that was about all they had going for them.

As far as go-go bars went, that was about it in Daylesford. There was Nine Inch Males, but that was a stripper bar, so, totally different. We always kept our briefs on and there was a very strictly enforced *look with your eyes, not with your hands* policy at The Tank Top.

There were also a couple of BDSM clubs in Daylesford. I'd never been to any of them, but I'd heard that The Cage was pretty good. But the town's undisputed kinky pièce de résistance was a place called Revolver. Apparently you needed some serious cash and status to even be considered for membership there.

Which is why I'd never been—I didn't have either.

I was particularly short on cash, at the moment. Hence the seven-tiered cake I had lugged over to The Tank Top with me. The same cake whose box Tristan was trying to pry open.

"Hey, stop that," I said, slapping his hand away. "This isn't for you. It's for later."

Sam blinked at me a few times and I realized I hadn't answered his question. What was I going to be using the cake for?

The short answer was, to make money. That was the answer to pretty much every question anyone asked me at the moment. My life was all about money and making as much of it as I could. Not for me, although, ever since hipsters had taken over the thrift shops, looking this cheap had started to get a lot more expensive.

No, all the money I made, once I'd covered rent and other necessities—food, bills, bubble gum—went to the bakery. I loved my grandparents with all of my heart, but they sucked when it came to managing money. The bakery hadn't turned a profit in years, and just getting by was no longer enough, not with rapacious developers swimming around the place like sharks in a *Jaws* movie.

(See, I even know big words, thank you very much.)

So I was all about the money, baby. It's why I worked four jobs. It's why I helped my grandparents out at the bakery at the crack of dawn most mornings. And it's why I had this massive cake up on the bar, and why Sam with his wide-eyed expression, and now Tristan with his, were both looking at me, waiting for me to say something.

"Well," I began, slowly building the drama because...well, why not? "As Tristan knows, I've had a run of bad luck lately." Tristan nodded knowingly. "Yeah, my routines haven't exactly gone smoothly."

"Can I ask what happened?" Sam said.

"Well, I had an issue with my Britney number. You know her song *Gimme More*? The one with the chorus that goes *gimme more, gimme gimme more* on loop?" They both nodded their heads. "Well, during it, I would have food thrown at me and I'd pretend to be devouring it. It was super hilarious, you know, this big boy pretending to gobble up all of this food."

"That's a little out there but...cool," Sam said, looking a little uncertain about what to make of me. A totally common issue for most people who had only just met me, nothing to worry about.

"Well, it was my idea, and I thought it was pretty cool," I said with a proud smile.

The routine had been empowering, funny, ridiculous, and super, super *sassy*.

"Why did it get canned?" Tristan asked.

"It got too expensive," I replied with a sigh.

That routine was by far my most popular number. It drew a massive crowd each week and earned me more in tips than dancing on the podium ever did.

"Was it a licensing issue with the song or something?" Sam asked.

"No, it was the food. We only had a small budget and we ran out of money for food."

A giggle escaped Sam's lips as his cheeks flushed red.

"It's okay to laugh, it is kinda funny," I said with a chuckle.

"What about your champagne glass number?" Tristan asked. "That used to be epic."

I flung my head back at the memory of the big champagne glass I used to roll around in while water poured down from the ceiling.

"The glass cracked. My crack made it crack."

This time there were giggles from Tristan and Sam *and* me.

I guess it all was pretty ludicrous, but it did leave me with a serious dilemma. I needed something else to replace my old routines, something that would bring in just as much, if not more, money than I was making before.

"So, what's the cake for?" Sam asked again.

"Erotic cake-sitting," I said matter-of-factly as I picked up the cake and put it in the fridge just behind the bar.

When I returned, Sam's mouth was gaped open and Tristan was sending major *what the fuck* vibes my way.

"What?" I asked, looking at both of them as I took the sunglasses off my head and pulled my messy hair back into a loose bun. "I've got a client lined up later tonight that requested it."

"Requested what, exactly?" Tristan asked slowly, his rich voice a mix of confusion and concern.

He was used to my batshit crazy shenanigans, but even I could admit, this was kind of next-level crazy. Even by my standards.

"Yeah, I haven't even heard of erotic cake-sitting before," Sam added softly.

"Yeah well, you know what they say about us G-A-Ys. We're generations ahead of yesterday." I added a finger click for extra effect.

"Still not answering the question, Nick," Tristan said, trying to hide his bemused smile.

"Well, it's kinda in the name, guys. Erotic cake-sitting," I repeated. "I'll be sitting on a cake...erotically."

A sound escaped from Tristan's throat, but I couldn't tell if it was a chuckle or something else.

"Are you being serious about this?" He narrowed his eyes at me.

"I am." The bar had rooms—we called them booths—where clients could request a private dance with their favorite boy. Or boys.

"You know Willie, right?" I asked, looking at Tristan.

He gave a nod. "He's a regular, been coming here for years. Since before I even started here," Tristan explained to Sam.

"So, like, since the '70s, basically," I added with a grin and was met with a middle finger from Tristan.

Sam let out a nervous giggle, looking like he wasn't entirely sure where to look, who to listen to, and what the fuck to make out of all of this.

"Well, I'm one of Willie's favorite boys—"

"Second favorite," Tristan interrupted.

"Whatever," I said, smiling. "One night, he and I were talking at the bar and he said that he was into sploshing."

"What's splashing?" Sam asked, his brows furrowed in even more confusion.

"No, not *splashing*," I corrected him. "Sploshing. It's when a person likes wet or messy play, usually with food or drinks. They like watching it happen or they like having it happen to them."

"Like what? I don't get it," Sam asked.

"It can be anything," I began. "Some people get turned on by seeing someone rub food over themselves, or spill a drink on themselves. Sometimes it happens clothed and other times it can happen naked. It all depends on the person, but it's a very visual thing for the person watching and it's a very tactile, sensory thing for the person doing it."

I could see Tristan and Sam nodding their heads, slowly taking it all in. When you're a go-go boy, you get a ton of crazy requests. And if you want to be a successful go-go boy, you quickly learn not to judge them—within reasonable limits, of course.

I'd been a go-go dancer for almost four years and had heard it all. From a guy wanting me to dance in a three-piece suit, to a request for me to do the running man and robot all night, to a request from a married couple where one guy only wanted me to dance for his husband, and not for him.

Hey, whatever made people happy—and, more importantly, happy to tip. I was down for pretty much anything.

Willie and I had been talking a couple of months back when he mentioned sploshing for the first time. Being a curious guy, I did some research online and we kept talking about it.

I got the all-clear from the bar owner, Mason Knight, who thought it sounded like a really cool idea. I had been doing private sploshing sessions for Willie, and two other clients, for the past month or so.

It had the added bonus of injecting some much-needed cash into my grandparents' bakery. The cakes themselves cost around six hundred dollars, that's why grandma put so much time and effort into them.

I just didn't know how to tell her that they had to be nicely decorated, that was all. It was all about the look of the cake and never the taste. Because no one ever actually ate the cake. That would just be unhygienic, and in any case, that wasn't part of the fantasy for these particular kinksters.

I had been doing the sploshing sessions in secret until I got my confidence up enough to share it with the other boys. It was becoming increasingly difficult trying to smuggle these huge-ass cakes into the bar, and believe me, there's no one better at smuggling huge-ass cakes than this booty-popping boy.

"So there you have it, guys. In addition to all my already impressive talent list, I am now also an erotic cake sitter."

"Nice," Tristan said, giving me an approving nod. His concerns seemed to have been allayed. "Make sure you add that to your business card."

"Ha, business card," Sam threw his head back, letting out a laugh. "Who even uses those anymore?"

At twenty-four, I usually didn't feel old...until I talked to a twenty-one-year-old. A *newly turned* twenty-one-year-old. Then I felt ancient.

On top of feeling like I belonged in a museum exhibit, I was hit with a heavy sadness that pummeled my chest as my head filled with the memory of the last person who had given me his business card.

CHAPTER TWO

STEEL

"Alright, alright," Stirling said as he dragged the back of his hand across his forehead, wiping the sweat on the side of his pants. His eyes darted between the simmering pan of deep red sauce and the handwritten piece of paper containing the meal's recipe on the countertop. Mikey stood a few feet away, his eyes glued to Stirling's every move.

Stirling's normally cool, calm, and steady demeanour had taken the night off. In its place was a Daddy desperately trying to perfect his boy's secret family recipe for bolognese. The weight of generations bore down on his wide shoulders. His face was stuck in a permanent, sweat-lined grimace.

"I've added the onions, stirred, now it's time for..." He picked the paper up and squinted at his bad handwriting.

"Glasses?" I suggested, raising a glass of wine to my lips.

Stirling shot me an evil look as Mikey approached him and

gently placed one hand on his shoulder. With the other, he picked up a spice jar from the counter.

"Oregano," he said in that sweet, warm voice of his.

"Thanks, baby," Stirling said, twirling around to face Mikey and planting a delicate kiss on his lips. Mikey closed his eyes, leaning into his Daddy's body.

My stomach let out a loud growl as I smiled, watching the loved-up couple. My chest bloomed with happiness, seeing my best friend looking—and being—so happy with his boy. Finally. He deserved it more than anyone. He and Mikey really were a perfect match.

"What did you have for lunch?" Stirling asked without looking up, carefully adding the oregano and stirring it into the bubbling sauce.

"I think he's talking to you," Mikey said as he lifted my glass to pour me a refill.

His big blue eyes, the same eyes that I had been hearing Stirling gush over like a teenager almost every day since they'd met, were filled with genuine happiness as he looked at me.

Mikey was such a good boy, exactly what Stirling needed in his first relationship with a younger guy. Seeing them together over the last six months had proven that to me, time and again.

I saw it even in the way they moved together in Stirling's small and previously completely unused kitchen. They had that natural flow that all good couples have. A silent understanding existed between them. They knew what to do and say at just the right time.

Stirling was nervous and more fussy than I'd seen him in a long time because it was his first time making Mikey's nonna's spaghetti recipe. It was good to see the man stepping out of his comfort zone, and it was even better seeing Mikey respond accordingly. He gave him space, he gave him time, and when needed, he gave him support. Or oregano, as the case might be.

Mikey was a good boy like that. Sensitive, attuned to his Daddy, confident in his own needs, and compliant when necessary. He made Stirling happier than I had ever seen him, and we'd been best friends for over twenty years.

I knew that winning the seemingly never-ending court case, and finally getting justice for his mom, was a huge relief for Stirling too, but it was nothing compared to what was blossoming in his heart for Mikey.

"Yeah, I skipped lunch today," I said, scratching the back of my neck. I braced for the grilling I knew was coming.

"Again?" Stirling's voice was low and thick with concern.

"Just going through a bit of a busy patch, that's all."

Stirling grumbled but I was saved by the sauce simmering over a little too high.

"Maybe you should turn down the heat...Daddy," Mikey breathed into his ear.

"I don't hear those words coming out of your mouth very often," Stirling let out a low laugh as he turned the heat down on the stove and stole a quick kiss from Mikey.

"Oh my god, get a room, you two."

Mikey saw me roll my eyes and laughed. "We don't need a room. We've got two houses between us."

Stirling's eyes met mine briefly and I knew what he was thinking. He was going to ask Mikey to move in with him, but was waiting for just the right moment to do it. Cooking Mikey's nonna's spaghetti bolognese for the first time, with me hanging on like a third wheel, was clearly not going to be it.

I didn't quite know when I got relegated to third-wheel status, but I was definitely feeling it. Running a law firm certainly didn't help. It wasn't just my career, it was my passion. I'd started it because I didn't want to do soulless corporate law. I wanted to actually help people and make a real difference. To use the justice system to do the good it was designed for, and all that goody-goody crap. But it wasn't crap to me. Despite the many, many shitshows happening in the world, I really did believe in justice.

It wasn't just the firm, though. I was probably using that as a cover, really, a way of avoiding the big gaping hole in my life. I was a Daddy without a boy. And while I was active in the Daylesford kink scene and went to Revolver frequently, it wasn't the same as having a relationship. Someone to share my life with.

Since my late twenties, I had felt a pull toward caregiver relationships. I'd had a few casual flings over the years, but nothing even remotely serious. I'd just never been able to find the right one, where there was that spark, that body-level attraction that transcended words because it came from a place deep inside.

Well, there was one boy I had met. Coincidentally, it was Mikey's best friend, Nick, but that was going nowhere fast. I pouted into my wine.

"So," Mikey said, looking in my direction, his blue eyes gleaming mischievously. "Are you looking forward to tonight?"

"You mean having dinner with my best friend and his lovely boy? Yes, I am." I hid my smile behind the wine glass.

I knew full well that wasn't what Mikey was asking, but if he wanted to draw something out of me, I'd make him work for it.

"That's nice," he said as his lips stretched into a wide smile. "And what about going out later?"

Bingo. He was fishing.

How I let Stirling rope me into this, I'd never know. I guess I had been burning the candle at both ends, so a night out sounded like a good idea. In theory.

But going out to The Tank Top, of all places? A heavy pit formed in my empty, growling stomach as I clenched my jaw at the thought of it.

Of him.

I'd definitely be seeing him tonight. There was no way Stirling and Mikey hadn't organised it for precisely that reason. They were as transparent as a sheet of glass, although why they were even bothering trying to get Nick and I into the same space, I had no idea. He'd probably find a way to escape, as he always did whenever we were near one another.

The guy clearly wasn't interested in me.

I'd given him my business card the night we met at my fortieth birthday party. I hadn't expected a call straight away, but given how well we had gotten on that night, I had expected a call at some stage.

He was unlike anyone I had ever met.

He was loud. He was opinionated. He was balls-to-the-wall funny. He had attitude seeping out of his pores, and his body...oh sweet Jesus, his body...

I never thought in my whole life that I would ever quote a John Mayer song, but his body truly was a wonderland. One I wanted to explore and get lost in, over and over and over again.

This will make me sound all sorts of douchey, and I really don't mean it in the douchey way, but I was a little surprised that he never called. I've never had a guy that I'd given my number to not call me. And let me tell ya, it sucked big-time balls.

I even took on the task of organizing Hudson's fortieth birthday party on a yacht, making sure to book Mikey and Nick as the naked butlers for the evening, just so I could see Nick again. He was fine for the first half of the evening. More than fine, actually. He was flirting and chatting away, and giving me as much shit as I gave him.

I absolutely loved it.

He didn't fawn all over me and he didn't seem to be impressed by my money or my success, which was refreshing. So many of the boys who were interested in me knew about my law firm, or had heard about how much money I had, or had seen me referred to as "Anderson Cooper's even hotter cousin" in *The Daylesford Times*, which had also named me one of Daylesford's Most Eligible Daddies—three years running.

But not Nick.

He didn't seem to care about any of that. When I was with him, it was like everything else faded away and it was just him...and just me.

He was never mean or rude, but he never skipped a beat in

serving it up to me. His cheeky comments, his cockiness, his preening. There was no way he could have known how much that turned me on.

By the end of Hudson's party on the yacht, something had changed in him. It was a seismic shift. He completely ignored me the next few times our paths crossed on the yacht, and despite seeing him a few times here and there as Stirling and Mikey started dating and our social circles mingled, he barely ever muttered more than a few words to me. Usually angry words.

It was enough to make even the most confident Daddy start to doubt himself.

"You're thinking about him, aren't you?" Stirling's voice stirred me from my thoughts.

I looked over and saw Mikey holding a deep plate while Stirling carefully poured the bolognese over the pasta, his tongue glued to the upper corner of his mouth in concentration.

"What? No," I said as I straightened out the front of my shirt. "What makes you say that?"

I couldn't help but be a little curious.

"Well, firstly, it's the fact that you know exactly who I'm talking about without me even saying his name."

Damn. Nick had burned himself into my brain so deeply that I'd just assumed Stirling had been talking about him. I sat up a little taller and squared my shoulders.

"And then there's that thing that your face does whenever you think about him."

Was there a limit on how many times a forty-year-old man could roll his eyes in one evening? I saw what he was doing here, and I didn't appreciate his attempts at cutesiness.

"And what might that be?" I asked, raising an eyebrow.

"Frowning," he replied, looking up from the plate and meeting my gaze square on.

That wasn't the answer I was expecting.

"Frowning?"

"Yeah, the type of frown I'd see you do in the courtroom when we were getting smashed by the defense team. The type of frown that really dives into your skin and brings out your deep wrinkles."

"Geez, okay, stop," I groaned. It came out louder than I had expected.

Maybe his words stung because they hit too close to home.

"Agreed," Mikey said as he held up the last empty plate to Stirling. "No more talking about wrinkles. That's not allowed here."

We all chuckled and I appreciated his attempt to lighten the situation, but there was no use in even pretending that would be the end of that conversation.

This wasn't like me at all. I wasn't the kind of guy who dwelled on things he couldn't change. If I couldn't do something about a situation, I'd move on. But with Nick, I couldn't do that. I was trapped between not being able to be with him, and yet at the same time, I couldn't seem to get him out of my head either.

Stirling motioned with his head and I followed him and Mikey over to the dining table.

"Mmm, this is delicious," I said as I put a forkful of pasta and bolognese into my mouth.

"It is," Mikey agreed with his mouth half full.

Stirling, meanwhile, was struggling to tame the long strands of pasta around his fork.

"Does it taste like your nonna's?" I asked, and Mikey's eyes widened immediately.

It was only when I saw his reaction that I realized what I had done. I didn't mean to put him on the spot like that, but thankfully, Stirling's mouth was still pasta-less and he was able to salvage the situation.

"No one could ever make it like Mikey's nonna can," he said.

Stirling Bishop. Daylesford's newest Daddy and the epitome of dinner table diplomacy.

"And no one can ever make it like my Daddy," Mikey said, and I was pretty sure I saw a whole bunch of animated hearts flutter out of his eyes and land inside Stirling's chest.

"So, you and Nick then, what's the deal?" Stirling asked as he finally forced a whole bunch of pasta—inelegantly—into his mouth.

I sighed. "Same as always...nothing. No deal. It's as if he hates me."

"He doesn't hate you." Mikey spoke, but I could hear the trepidation in his words.

"He doesn't?" I asked a little too quickly.

"Well, uh, I mean...hate's a strong word."

"Oh, so he just casually dislikes me then?" I slumped back into my chair.

"No, he doesn't dislike you either," Mikey added after some careful thought.

A feeling of hope rose in my chest, which was pretty pathetic considering it was based on the guy not disliking me. It's never a good sign when you plant your hope flag in double-negative territory.

"Honestly," Mikey said, putting down his fork and spoon and looking at me. "I just think you guys need to spend some time together. Get to know one another. I think you'd really like each other. More than just *casually* like each other," he added with a cheeky grin.

"Well that sounds good in theory, Mikey, but the guy acts like he's allergic to me. Whenever I show up somewhere, he always seems to disappear. It will be the same thing tonight, I can guarantee it."

"Well, there is something you can do about that," Mikey said.

He looked over at Stirling, whose face was as blank as mine. Stirling shot me his *I have no idea where this is going* look, so at least I knew the two of them weren't conspiring against me.

"Oh yeah?" I said, wiping the corners of my mouth with a napkin. "And what might that be, Mikey?"

"Request a private dance with him." He said it like it was the most obvious thing in the world.

"A private dance?" I asked.

"Can you even do that?" Stirling added, his thick brows pinching together.

Mikey's laugh filled the entire room. "I thought you guys were like the Daddy Council of Daylesford. Shouldn't you know these sorts of things?"

I shuffled in my seat.

"In my defense," I said, trying my best not to sound like a lawyer, but not sure if it was working. "I don't normally hang out at The Tank Top. I'm more of a Revolver type of Daddy."

"Relax, I was just kidding," Mikey said, his whole face lit up in a playful smile. "Yes, you can book a private dance with him, and that way, there's no chance he'll run away."

"He won't mind?" I asked. The last thing I wanted to do was to make Nick feel like I was cornering him.

"Nope, he's totally in control," Mikey replied confidently. "If he's uncomfortable with anything, he can end the dance whenever he wants. But he won't. Trust me, Steel. It'll be a good thing. Besides, he really needs the money right now."

A darkness wiped the smile off Mikey's lips, replaced with a look of guilt, as if he had said something he shouldn't have.

"What do you mean?" I asked. A protective sense had been triggered in my chest and I wanted to find out more.

"Nothing, I shouldn't have said...I just...If you want to talk to him, Steel, that's how you could do it. That's all I'm saying."

"Nice save, baby," Stirling said as he cupped Mikey's hand in his.

We ate in silence for a while, my mind consumed with thoughts of the boy I hadn't been able to get out of my head for more than six months. The boy who seemed so interested and into me at first, but now couldn't stand to breathe the same air as me.

The boy who I would get a private dance from tonight and find out definitively—one way or another—just what his problem with me was.

CHAPTER THREE

NICK

The Tank Top was packed and pumping as I grabbed Mason's outstretched hand and lowered myself down off the podium. I was covered in sweat, glitter, and body oil, and I had a truckload of dollar bills stuffed down my fluro-pink boxer briefs and hanging out of my faded brown leather cowboy boots. Even though Mason was the bar owner and probably had a million other things to be doing, he was always there to help one of his boys get off the podium safely.

"Great set tonight," he said, helping me scoop up a few errant bills that had fallen off the podium.

"What can I say?" I shouted over the throbbing music. "I know how to whip the crowd into a frenzy."

He smiled and handed me a bottle of water as I started to make my way through a throng of equally sweaty—though fully clothed—men when I felt a hand pinch my right butt cheek.

"Hey, asshole," I said, turning around, about to serve this jerk a mouthful, when I saw who it was. I bit down on my lip to hide my smile.

"Hey, asshole, yourself," Mikey said with a giggle as he leaned in for a hug. "Is this how we're greeting each other now?"

"Careful, I'm all sweaty," I said, not wanting to ruin Mikey's outfit.

He was dressed in his usual preppy-yet-casually-cool style: ridiculously tight black pants that looked like they were painted on and a light blue polo shirt.

After my many, many, *many* repeated requests, he was finally lightening his hair from that god-awful jet black he'd sported since breaking up with his dirtbag ex, Brian, and getting it back to his cute blond self. God wanted us all to be blond. It's even in the bible—somewhere near the back. Mikey's hair was a dark ashy blond at the moment, a compromise that would have to do for the time being.

"I don't care about a little sweat," he said, brushing the comment off with all the confidence of a boy who had found his forever Daddy.

I was beyond happy that my best friend was in a good, healthy, and—from the little titbits I had managed to pry from him—incredibly sexual relationship. I could literally, spontaneously, burst from pure happiness for him.

Stirling was a good man and exactly the kind of Daddy that Mikey deserved. Strong, steady, dependable...and hung like a donkey, or racehorse, or whatever animal it was that had a massive cock. After picking three total tools in a row for boyfriends, Mikey had struck it fourth-time lucky.

"And where is your magnificent Daddy?" I asked as we pushed our way through the backstage door and made our way down the short white-bricked hallway to the changing room.

"He's at the bar."

The words sounded perfectly innocent and normal, but the beauty of knowing someone since before your voice broke was that you could pick up on just the slightest *tone*. It was barely more than the tiniest of tiny inflections, but I instantly knew Mikey was up to something.

Before I could press it any further, he asked, "So, what's happening in the old love life department, Nicky boy?"

"Ha," I snorted as I toweled myself down. "What love life? I mean, unless you can get married to money."

"Things still tough at the bakery?" he asked.

"Yeah," I said, drawing a deep breath and throwing the towel away. "But when life gave Beyoncé lemons, she made *Lemonade*. And that's exactly what I intend to do."

I put on an old faded green tank top and a pair of red short-shorts. Together with my mid-length cowboy boots, they made my legs look ah-mazing. And my butt? Don't even get me started.

I had an hour until my next dance set, which was a pretty decent break, and now that my best friend was here, it was time for us to indulge in our customary old-as-time-itself tradition—shots at the bar.

"That's a really good attitude," Mikey said, and that tone was back, but bigger this time. Much more noticeable, like he wasn't trying to hide it as much anymore.

I was about to open the door back to the main floor of the bar, but stopped and turned to look at him.

"Okay, what is up, Mikey Harrison? I know you, I know that voice, and I know I'm probably not going to like it. Right?" I walked slowly toward him as he stepped backward, away from me.

"What? No," he said, trying to cover up what his eyes were giving away. "You'll—you'll love it."

"Ah ha!" I exclaimed, planting my index finger perilously close to the tip of his nose. "I knew there was an *it* and you just confirmed it. Now spill, Mikey boy."

"Shoot," he said, closing his eyes.

I laughed at how innocent that word sounded, but I folded my arms across my beefy chest as well, letting him know I was serious. There would be no shots at the bar until I had the full 4-1-1.

"I just want you to be happy, Nick," he said.

"What are you talking about? I am happy." Kinda. Sorta. Well, maybe not really happy, but I mean really, who's actually happy these days?

"Are you sure?" Mikey asked, and I could tell he wasn't picking up what I was putting down.

"Yes, I am," I said with the widest smile and happiest-sounding voice I could muster. "I am totally, one hundred percent happy. Deffers."

Mikey scrunched up his nose. "Deffers?"

"I slept with an Aussie guy a few months back. It's short for *definitely*," I said, by way of explanation. "And see, I am happy. I mean, who wouldn't be happy after sleeping with an Aussie guy? They're fab-u-lous in bed."

I was about to launch into one of my world-famous accents when Mikey spoke in a torrent stream of anguished breath.

"Please don't do an accent. Your accents are terrible. All of them. Every single one of them. I know you think they aren't, but they are."

He winced, and covered his face, as if getting ready for me to hit him.

"Mikey, I'm shocked," I said with an evil smile. Evil, because I knew full well that he was right, my accents were shockingly bad, but also because I had successfully sidestepped his question.

Or so I thought.

"I just, I just want you to be happy in the same way that I'm happy with Stirling," he said.

"Shoot."

There weren't many subjects that I didn't like to talk about, or topics that were off limits, but my disaster of a love life came pretty close.

Don't get me wrong, I had guys coming out of my ears. Wait,

that didn't sound right. What I meant was that ever since Daddies, bears, cubs, otters and big boys in general had become a thing—and a wildly popular thing at that—I had my fair share of interested guys.

Sure, I may have had eleven other boys to compete with here at The Tank Top, but I regularly got the most tips and was very highly requested for private dances. There would always be men who were into slimmer guys, or purely muscular guys, or guys who shaved every single last hair that wasn't on top of their heads, but a lot of guys liked the BBE—big boy energy—that I gave off.

"I'm not talking about your work, Nick," Mikey said as if he were inside my head, reading my mind. "I know you're super popular and you deserve to be. One *thousand* percent. But...there's more to life than just work and the attention you get from guys at work."

I sighed. "You realize this conversation means we're going to have to have double shots now, don't you?"

He let out a small smile which softened his face even more.

"Nick." He didn't need to say anything else.

We both knew it. I was a disaster to date because, well...I was a lot. Like, *a lot* a lot. Too much for most guys to handle, anyway. Some could handle part of me, but never all of me.

Guys who liked my body, didn't like my loud mouth. Guys who liked my attitude and spunkiness, didn't like my body. But I was a complete-package kinda guy and I wasn't going to make myself smaller in any way, for anyone.

"Steel's here tonight," Mikey said, although he could have just picked me up and shoved me against the brick wall. His words had the same effect.

"What...what...what do you mean Steel is here?"

"Uh, which part would you like me to repeat?" he asked half-jokingly, scratching the back of his head nervously.

"Did you guys run into him?" I asked as my ribs tightened and squeezed the air out of my lungs.

"Not exactly." That tone in his voice was back again. Unmissable and unmistakable this time.

"Okay, what does *that* mean?" I asked, glaring at Mikey.

"Steel came over for dinner at Stirling's place tonight and we came out here together. To see you, Nick. Steel wants to see you."

My head flung back as I let out an exasperated sigh.

"Ever thought that maybe I don't want to see him?" My words hung heavily in the air between us, while Mikey looked like he was considering what I had said.

"But why not?" he finally pressed. I could tell he wasn't going to give this one up anytime soon. "He's Stirling's best friend, Nick. They've known each other forever."

I huffed. "Say it in a way that I would understand."

Mikey shook his head with a smile and paused for a moment before his eyes lit up like Christmas trees.

"Stirling and Steel became friends when Destiny's Child still had four members."

"Wow, that is a long time," I said after a few moments, carefully considering how long ago that really was.

"Yes, it is," Mikey said seriously. "That means he's a good guy, Nick. Stirling wouldn't have been friends with the guy for that long if he weren't."

"No, he's not, Mikey," I sighed. I didn't want to say it, but he'd cornered me and given me no other choice. "Steel is a jerk."

An exasperated look flashed across Mikey's face. I'd seen that look a thousand times before.

"What makes you say that? Why do you have it in your head that he's a jerk? What has the man ever done to you apart from drool and practically fall all over himself every time you walk into his line of sight?"

"Look," I said as I grabbed Mikey by the shoulders. "Like you said, he's your boyfriend's best friend. I don't want to talk shit about him. But I know what I know. And Steel Crawford is not a nice guy. Now can we puh-lease go out and have some shots at the bar?"

But Mikey wasn't giving up. He stepped back and placed both hands on his hips.

"This isn't like you, Nick," he said. "You don't normally judge people like this. I don't know what you know, or what you *think* you know, but take it from me—Steel Crawford is a nice guy. In fact, he's one of the nicest."

I sighed. I didn't want to argue with my best friend, so I caved.

"Okay, okay. I'm open to the idea that Steel isn't the biggest asshole in the world. Now can we please go and get a little drunk?"

He must have heard the pleading in my voice, because he stepped in, nodded, and gave me a tight squeeze.

"I love you, and I just want you to be happy," Mikey said into my ear.

"I love you too, and I want me to be happy, too," I replied.

"Just give him a chance, okay?"

How could I resist those baby blues?

"Sure, Mikey boy," I said as I ran my fingers through his still unsatisfactorily colored hair.

I meant it, even though they were hollow words. I'd successfully spent most of Mikey and Stirling's relationship avoiding Steel. I'd become quite good at it. It was practically a game at this point. A game I always managed to win.

The Tank Top was a big bar. Tonight, it was packed full of people. There was no way in hell I would have to spend more than a few seconds with Steel. If we did run into each other, I'd say a quick 'hi' and then scoot my cute self off before I got hooked into exchanging any more words with the man.

"Hey, Nick, there you are," Tristan said as he popped his head around the corner. "You've just been booked for a private dance. Room three. Starting in ten minutes, okay?"

"Great, thanks, Tristan," I said, rubbing my hands in glee as he disappeared.

A private dance was guaranteed money, plus tips.

This was going to be a good night. I could feel it.

I was going to pull in some serious cash with a private dance as well as another erotic cake-sitting session I had booked for later in the night. I was going to have a shot—or five—with my best friend in the whole wide world. And I was going to forget about everything else that was going on with the bakery and my non-existent love life.

"Have we still got time for a quick shot at the bar?" Mikey asked.

"Oh, we do, Mikey boy," I said, wrapping my arm around his waist as we headed to the bar. "We deffers do."

CHAPTER FOUR

STEEL

I ran my hand nervously along the side of the chair in the dim private booth. I looked down at my fingers, tapping away furiously, a sign of the stress that permeated throughout my entire body. Maybe this wasn't such a great idea after all.

I curled my fingers into a fist, determined to stop the rattling sound echoing off the walls and quiet my mind, as well. I needed to focus here.

What was I trying to do? What did I want to achieve? Most importantly, why had I not been able to get this guy, who'd been ignoring me for months, out of my head?

That last question was for another time. But as I looked around the room, which couldn't have been more than eight feet wide, with two comfortable black leather armchairs and a dancing podium at the front, my mind was desperately scrambling, trying to find some logic to my madness.

Ultimately, I just wanted to know why. Why he was ignoring me whenever we saw each other, why he was acting like he hated me, and why he had never called. Forget the dancing, although that would be a very pleasant distraction. No, I needed Nick to sit down next to me and just talk, not run away like he always did.

I had no idea why this was bothering me so much. Why hadn't I just taken the hint? I mean, it wasn't like he was ever subtle about his displeasure at my mere presence. Why hadn't I just moved on?

Just as my mind turned to how I saw the conversation between us going, music started to blare from the speakers. The dim lights on the walls around me faded to black, the same way they did at the movies, and the dancing podium in front of me lit up in a neon red and blue hue.

As the beat kicked in, Nick's outline appeared on the podium. He was silhouetted in black, striking a pose. I looked around. He must have come in from a secret door at the side of the booth that I couldn't see.

He began to move in time with the music. Short, sharp, sexy movements. A hip rock, a shoulder lean, a booty move that had my eyes gaping open and my tongue practically hanging out of my mouth. Fuck me, he was sexy.

I could feel my cock thickening in my pants. I palmed it down. This wasn't Revolver or a sex club. This was a go-go bar and the staff member who booked this dance for me went to great lengths to ensure I knew the rules.

As with most things, it boiled down to consent. If I wanted to touch, if I wanted him to dance a certain way, if I wanted to talk, I had to ask first and get his permission. The only two things that weren't allowed were nudity and sex. They were hard limits.

Which was fine with me, because I wasn't here for that. I had to remind myself of that, though, as my dick throbbed in my pants. The more Nick danced, the more his moves distracted me from my purpose, why I was here.

I wanted to talk to him. And I would...after just a few more moves.

I was transfixed by his body. I'd never seen anything like it before. He looked like a teddy bear and bodybuilder rolled into one. It was an intriguing, intoxicating combination.

I mean, the guy had some serious muscles. His biceps were bigger than mine and his thighs were the size of tree trunks. But then he had a soft, big belly. It was round and hairy and from the second I saw it, I wanted nothing more than to slide my hands all over it.

At that moment, Nick stepped off the podium and brought that enticing body tantalizingly close to me. He placed his finger on my shoulder as he strutted around me, slowly letting me soak all of him in.

My heart was racing faster than the music and I knew I had to stop this. He obviously couldn't see my face and I knew he probably wouldn't have the best reaction to seeing me. But damn, just his finger on my shoulder sent a hot spark shooting down my spine and straight to the tip of my hard cock.

"Nick, it's Steel," I said, abruptly standing up.

"Oh shit." He took a step back and for a moment I was worried he would fall over, but he quickly steadied himself. "What are you doing here?"

I could hear the irritation in his voice.

"I want to talk to you, Nick. Are you able to turn the music off?"

He turned around and it looked like he was about to march out of the booth in anger. But instead, he knelt down and the music turned off. A moment later, the lights came back to life, bathing the booth in a warm yellow glow.

He walked back over to me, placed a hand on his hip, and cocked his head to the side.

"Care to explain what the fuck is going on?"

His shoulder-length hair looked like silk in the dim light, but his brown eyes were like two tornadoes coming straight for me.

"Can we talk? Please?" I pointed to the empty chair beside me. "I mean, if that's allowed."

"It's not the most unusual request I've received," he said, and the two tornadoes softened slightly...into storms. He was still pissed, but I felt I had just the slightest opening. That was all I needed.

"Wait a sec," he said as he turned around and left the booth.

Or maybe I was wrong. I had no idea how to read the guy. Before my mind could start racing again, he returned, closing the door behind him firmly. He had a navy blue dressing gown in his hands which he quickly wrapped around himself before he plonked down in the chair next to me.

"You want to talk," he said, arching his eyebrows with more attitude than I ever thought two eyebrows could muster. "So talk."

God, I loved it when he was like this. All cockiness and attitude. What the hell was wrong with me? Clearly, I needed help. But I had his attention so I had to go for it.

"Nick," I began, my mind suddenly going blank. Suddenly I was unable to string a sentence together. "What's going on?"

"What do you mean?"

He pursed his lips into a thin line.

"I think you know what I mean," I said, shooting him a knowing look which he ignored. "I thought we got on well the first night we met, at my fortieth birthday party."

"Yeah, we did," he replied casually, absorbed in the finer details of his fingernails which must have been fascinating, because he wasn't looking up from them at all.

"And then, on the yacht at Hudson's party, it was great to see you again," I said.

He looked up at me, his brown eyes still brewing.

"Yeah, it was okay to see you again, I guess," he half-spoke, half-huffed.

"And then ever since that party, you've just been so...weird toward me. You practically run at the sight of me but if we do end up talking, you always sound like you're angry at me and then you find a way of disappearing a few seconds later. Have I done something to upset you?"

There, I'd said it. After all these months, we were finally talking and the issue was on the table.

He let the words hang there, suspended in mid-air between us. His face was blank and he was trying to play it cool, but his chest was heaving. Something was definitely going on inside of him.

"My only problem with you, Steel," he said as he leaned in closer, "is that you're a jerk."

"What?" I rocked back in my chair. Why on earth would he think that? I was genuinely shocked. "Why do you think I'm a jerk, Nick?"

He stood up and walked a couple of feet. He kept looking away from me as he spoke.

"I heard what you said at the party."

"Hudson's party, on the yacht?" I asked. He nodded. "Did I say something to you?"

"No," he said, turning around, and for the first time I didn't see anger in his eyes, just hurt. "I overheard you talking to someone."

"Well, I talked to a lot of people that night," I said. "What exactly did you overhear?"

"You were up on the top deck talking to some guy, it wasn't one of your close friends, and you said..." His voice trailed off as he looked down at the floor. He shuffled his feet and looked like he was battling something within himself.

"What did I say, Nick?" I tried to keep my voice low and gentle, but I was determined to find out.

"You were talking to the guy about someone else and you called them a 'big, fat, stupid baby.'"

Nick crashed into the seat beside me and folded his arms across his chest. I was desperately scouring my memory from that night, trying to place the conversation, who I'd been talking to, and who I could have said that about.

Then I remembered, faintly, my conversation with an old

colleague, Arthur. We were talking about someone we both used to work with, a total dick of a guy who was, in actuality, a big, fat, stupid baby.

"I think I remember something," I said, desperately trying to piece together the small fragments of memory I had from that evening about five months ago. Nick's head snapped to attention. "But I don't see why you would get so upset with me just because I called someone a big, fat, stu..."

Oh shit.

I looked at Nick and his eyes were tornadoes again.

"Nick, I didn't mean it like that. It's just an expression. A stupid, stupid expression," I pleaded. "I didn't even think about what the words meant when I was saying them. I didn't mean it like that, I swear to you."

Nick tapped his fingers on the armrest of the chair as he looked at me, studying my face, looking for signs that he could either trust me or discount me as a complete liar—in addition to being a jerk. I couldn't tell what he was thinking. He wasn't giving anything away. His face was blank, his eyes glazed.

I broke the silence. "I like you, Nick. I like your attitude. Your confidence. Your sense of humor. All of it."

I frowned as I looked over at him. His face wasn't moving, it was still blank. He wasn't responding to anything I was saying.

"Great, so you like my wonderful personality," he said, rolling his eyes into the back of his head.

"Yeah, I do actually," I replied indignantly. "And I think you're fucking hot, too."

That got his attention as he sat up straighter in his seat.

"I think you have an incredible body. I love all of it. I like your brown eyes that shine with mischief when you talk. I like the way your hair bounces when you walk. I like your big arms and your wide shoulders. And that fucking belly," I dropped my head back and let out a deep moan. "You have no idea how much I want to touch that belly, Nick. How much I want to touch all of your body."

His face softened, but I still couldn't tell what he was thinking.

"Well, you can't do that here. Touch me, that is," he said quietly.

"I know, I know. I've been informed of the rules and I intend to follow them," I said.

"Here," he repeated.

"Huh?"

"You can't touch me *here*, but we can always leave *here*."

He tilted his head down and shot me such a filthy look I thought I would instantaneously combust.

"Well, let's go then," I said, getting up, not missing a beat.

My chest was swollen with heat and my cock was, well, swollen—and aching with a need for release.

I wanted him. I wanted Nick Macklin so fucking much. I wanted those big brown eyes staring into me as I plowed into him. I wanted to run my fingers through his hair as I kissed him rough. I wanted to run my hands, my lips, my tongue over that big beautiful belly of his and let the taste of his skin linger in my mouth.

I wanted it all, and this was my chance. I was going to take it. He got up and stood next to me. We were chest to chest, face to face.

"Just sex, no talking," he said.

His warm sweet breath hit my face. It had just the faintest whiff of strawberry bubblegum. I licked my lips.

"Yeah, okay, whatever. Just sex." I would have agreed to anything he said.

"I have one more client." He placed his hand on my shoulder and it sent an electric bolt through me. "I can be at your place straight after that?"

"Sure."

"Give me your business card," he said with a wry, seductive smile.

"Just make sure you use it this time." I fished it out of my wallet and handed it to him.

"Oh, I will," he said, grabbing the card and toying with it playfully between his fingers as he walked away.

The sweet strawberry scent remained in the air as I stood there, alone in the private booth with the biggest hard-on of my entire life.

CHAPTER FIVE

NICK

Me: *Well, I did what you asked.*
Mikey: *What's that?*
Me: *I'm giving Steel a chance.*

I let out a smile, imagining Mikey's face as he read my text. He'd either be confused by it or his eyes would be bulging out of his head. Or both.

Mikey: *Should I be scared...?*

I was in the backseat of an Uber on my way over to Steel's place. I'd finished my sploshing session with Willie and had two more shots with Tristan and Sam at the bar. I was horny as hell after what Nick had told me in the booth, and ready, willing, and able to make one giant mistake.

Well, actually, I'd already made one mistake earlier with Steel.

Yes, I had an issue with what I'd heard him say, but it wasn't just those words that I found so hurtful. That was only one part of it. But I wasn't ready to deal with the rest of it. At least, not yet. I'd deal with *that* once I figured things out a bit better in my own head, first.

Me: *No need to be scared. Everything will be fine.*
Mikey: *Are you sure?*

No.

If I was sure, my hands wouldn't be shaking like they were. But there was no need for Mikey to worry.

Me: *Deffers *smiley face emoji**

The driver pulled up out front of a massive apartment block right on the bay. I got out and made my way to the top floor, because of course Steel would live in the penthouse.

The long elevator ride gave me a chance to think. I closed my eyes to let some seriously good thinking happen. This was just sex. I repeated it approximately four hundred and thirty-two times just so that I wouldn't forget it.

Just sex. Nothing more and nothing else.

Because Steel was still kind of a jerk. He may not have meant what he said at the yacht party—and I believed that he didn't, people said stuff without thinking about what it actually meant all the time—but it still didn't change all the *other* stuff. But that was just as much on me as it was on him, I guess.

And that's why this just had to be sex. No feelings, no entanglement, no talking. Well, maybe some dirty talking was allowed. I was always open to expanding my catchphrase library. But nothing else.

And a one-time-only thing, too. Deffers a one-time-only thing. I didn't do repeats, because repeats led to feelings, and feelings led to entanglement. I didn't want any entanglements, especially with him.

The elevator doors opened and there he stood.

A vision.

A vision in white. He'd gotten changed and was wearing long white pants that clung to his muscled legs, what looked like a white cashmere sweater over his massive torso, and he was barefoot. Because of course the man had to look like a fucking GQ cover model while I was silently praying that I had managed to wash all of the cake out of my crack.

"You made it," he said with a smile as he outstretched his arms. The whiteness of everything he was wearing made his two rows of perfect teeth sparkle even more.

"Well, yeah, I made it," I said, not sure if I was going for casually cool or casually dismissive.

All of a sudden, I wasn't feeling as sure of myself as I normally was. It was the talking, it had to be the talking. We needed to fast forward to the sex part. Like, now.

"Can I take your..." he began and I handed him my bag without even thinking.

That wasn't what I'd wanted to do. I was perfectly capable of carrying my own bag. He placed it by the coat rack and indicated for me to step in.

The apartment that spread out before me was crazy. It was all open plan, and my eyes were immediately drawn to the floor-to-ceiling windows that looked out over the entire city. The lights shimmered outside and it made me think of Christmas, for some reason.

"You live here?" I asked and regretted it immediately.

Think, stupid brain—think, of course he lives here.

Steel smiled politely, thankfully ignored my stupid question, and asked, "Can I get you something to drink?"

"Do you have water?"

I winced again at the stupidity of what was coming out of my mouth. The man had taps, of course he had water. My mouth was dry and my brain was clearly in meltdown mode.

This had to stop. This whole *he says something and looks breathtakingly amazing and then I stumble over my words like a klutz* thing, like...well, Mikey. No, this couldn't keep going.

I wasn't here to take in the views. I wasn't here to drink water from a tap. I was here to have sex. With a super hot, silver fox, half-jerk, white-wearing vision of a man. Plain and simple.

"Would you like still or sparkling water?" he asked.

I said nothing. I just looked into those light blue eyes of his, eyes that looked as inviting as a swimming pool that I wanted to dive head first into.

"Shut up," I said as I closed the gap between us.

"You shut up," he replied, a devilish sparkle lighting up his face.

"Why don't we both shut up?" I said with a sassy head snap.

"Wait, that doesn't make any..."

Before he could finish, my lips smashed into his. I was here and I was hungry. Hungry for him. It took him barely a moment until he grabbed my face and pulled me in even closer, his thick, hard cock pressed into my hip.

I let out a small groan and my lips parted. He took that as an invitation as his tongue stormed into my mouth. I wasn't the only one who was hungry as Steel ravaged my mouth. His hands felt like they were all around me, dragging through my hair, running down my arms, cinching me tight around my waist.

I loved it. I loved every second of being enveloped by this man. He gently pulled my head back and attacked my neck with his teeth and tongue. The wet, warm pressure lit up my skin with tingles of pleasure. I felt giddy. Lightheaded. Like I would fall, but when I did, I knew he would catch me.

"Bedroom. Now."

His warm, minty-fresh breath filled my nostrils as we kissed our way over to one side of his apartment. The bedroom door was open and we stumbled our way through it. Somehow, his expert hands had gotten me almost naked while he remained fully clothed.

"Hey, no fair," I said as I placed both hands on his chest to create some space between us. "You need to get naked, too."

"Oh, I will," he leaned back into me and kissed me hard. "But first, let me enjoy watching you."

"What?" I stepped back sharply. "Just because I'm a go-go dancer, you think I'm yours to watch or something?"

"What? No, shit, sorry. I didn't mean..."

I erupted in laughter at his cute reaction. "Steel, I'm just teasing you. It's alright."

His face went through a hundred different expressions before landing on a conciliatory smile.

"I like you, Nick Macklin." He practically growled the words and I swear there must have been an invisible, silent earthquake in Daylesford, because I almost fell off my feet.

"Yeah?" I stepped backward to the bed as I ran my hand down my chest and across the top of my briefs. His eyes were locked on me, on my every movement. I ran my hand along my belly and I could feel the heat emanating from him. I could tell he would have preferred that to be his hand, and I wanted that too. But first, I wanted to tease him.

I ran my fingers along my pecs. I took two fingers into my mouth and wet them, and then in a slow circle, rubbed around my swollen purple-pink nipples. All the while, Steel's gaze was fixed on me as he was taking off his white pants, his white cashmere sweater, and the white shirt underneath it, leaving him standing there in just a pair of white boxer briefs. Because of course the man would be color coordinated down to his underwear.

And holy hell, if I thought the man was a vision before, wearing just his briefs, he was a Greek statue come to life. He didn't look real. In the dim shadows that danced across the walls of his bedroom, and with the outside twinkling of lights shining in through the windows, he looked like something out of this world.

His body was perfectly proportioned, every line and angle perfectly sculpted. His square jaw, his broad shoulders, his wide chest—it all looked so hard and appealing, I couldn't wait to bite into it. I may have been a big boy myself, but that didn't mean that I didn't appreciate the sight of a classically handsome man.

The only thing that was out of proportion was the massive bulge straining the front of his briefs. How his cock hadn't burst through the material was a miracle. It looked like he had stuffed a toy giraffe down there.

Slowly, he made his way toward me. I took a step back and fell into his bed. It was so big and so sturdy that it hardly moved—*that* would come in very handy a little later.

He stood over me, his body a tower of tanned muscles, hard lines, and moody shadows. His light blue eyes dragged up and down my body, his eyelids heavy with desire.

I slowly edged my way up the bed, pulling myself up by my elbows. I was moving away, but really, I was inviting him closer.

A smirk scrawled across his lips.

"You want me to chase you?" The thick rumble in his voice vibrated through my groin and my cock twitched in my briefs. We both saw the movement at the same time.

"Think you can catch me?" I teased, inching away from him and closer to the dark gray headboard at the top of the bed.

"Yeah," he said as his fingers wrapped themselves around my ankles. "I don't think catching you should be too much of a problem."

His fingers grazed upward along my leg, igniting my skin with an electric pulse.

"You might be able to catch me," I said as my head touched the headboard. "But can you keep me, Steel Crawford?"

His fingers pressed my thighs apart and he cupped my cock and balls in his hands.

"I don't know," he said, looking up at me. The light from outside hit his eyes, illuminating them with pure lust. "But I'll try my damndest."

The room was silent except for the drumming of my heartbeat, which I was sure he could hear, too. We were back here again, this whole stupid talking thing. Every time he spoke, he pierced further and further into me.

First, he was less of a jerk than I'd thought. Now, he was ten times hotter than I could have imagined he would be. And yeah, maybe I'd fantasized about how he'd look naked and towering over me once or twice.

He squeezed my cock and balls through my briefs and my head rocked back against the headboard. His pressure was firm. It hurt a little, but in a good way. I looked back at him and he swooped down, stuck his tongue out, and pressed it against the moistness that had formed on my briefs. He sucked at it ever so lightly. The slurping sound he made tore through my body.

I had no idea that silver fox Steel Crawford, one of Daylesford's top power Daddies, a super successful lawyer who ran his own firm, would be so...dirty.

Filthy.

Super fucking hot.

"Fuck me," I breathed, pushing my cock further into his warm palm. I was done with talking and I was done with teasing. I needed him inside me. Right now.

"Turn around. I want you on your hands and knees," he growled, and I was there, in position and waiting, before he had even grabbed the condoms and lube from the bedside drawer.

He pulled my briefs halfway down my thighs. He was being a little rough—and I liked it. My heart was thumping against my chest and I could feel my hole twitching with hunger for him.

"Do you want me to take my briefs off? I'll have to move," I said as I looked over my shoulder at him.

"Shut up."

The words smacked the air between us with a delicious, dirty crack. Worked for me.

I felt a wet, lubed up finger against me, playing with the sensitive skin around my entrance. It was cold and raw and sent a shiver through me. Feeling the way my body responded to his touch, he rubbed his other hand across my lower back and let out a delicate, soothing *shhhhh*. It calmed me instantly.

His finger entered me as my breath caught in my throat. He was sliding it in and out, loosening me up to get me ready. There was a reassuring thoughtfulness to his movement. I liked it.

He added another finger, then another, both slicked with lube, stretching me even wider. I let out a gasping moan.

"You okay?" he whispered.

"Yes," I panted back.

"You ready?" he asked, and I knew he would have stopped if I had said no.

But there was no way in hell I was saying that. I was ready, I was more than ready.

"Fuck me, Steel," I said as I fell down onto my elbows and rested my forehead against the firm mattress, lifting my ass higher into the air behind me.

His thick, long cock entered me in one slow, solid push, squeezing all the air out of my lungs and filling me with a burning hot sensation.

His balls pressed against my ass and he steadied himself by digging his fingers into my hips. The feeling of warmth and fullness flushed throughout my whole body and I felt like I was soaring through the sky.

"Fuck me," I begged.

He complied. Fucking me in slow, steady strokes at first, before building up the pace and the rhythm until the sounds of sex—his balls slapping against my ass and our moans—filled the air. I was getting close, and I could feel his balls tightening, too.

And then a hand grazed my lower belly. It was the lightest

touch, almost like a feather, but it was divine. Pure bliss. Steel was fucking me with all of his strength while stroking my belly so gently. It sent us both over the edge at the same time, and I wasn't even touching myself. Holy shit, how was this even happening?

Our bodies crashed and rocked against each other as he let out a deep, primal roar. My cock spasmed on its own, moving only in response to Steel's body against mine, as it let out rope after rope of release.

The sensation finally subsided. We were both covered with sweat as he gently pulled out of me. I flipped over onto my back and he was there beside me a second later, our unsteady breathing the only sound in the entire apartment.

"That was..." he began.

"Incredible," I said, without even blinking. Or thinking.

He looked over at me and played with a strand of hair that had fallen onto my shoulder. He smiled at me and then snuggled into my heaving chest.

"You taste like cake," he said, and I smiled as I ran my fingers through his silver mane.

CHAPTER SIX

STEEL

"You've never been with a big boy, have you?" Nick called after me as I got up to get us some towels so we could clean up a bit. Our bodies were covered in sweat and my lips tasted like icing sugar. Not that I was complaining.

"I hope that's not an indictment of my performance," I said with a half laugh as I returned from the bathroom with two wet cloths.

I sat down on the bed and looked at Nick. His face was so soft and smooth. It had an almost innocent quality to it. Almost. It glistened with a thin layer of post-sex sweat. He was the most wondrous creature I'd ever laid eyes on.

"I've dated all kinds of boys. Different shapes, sizes, ages, colors...I'm not judgmental in any way," I said.

"I'm not saying you are," he said, sitting up. He reached for the cloth, but I shook my head.

"May I?" I asked.

He cocked his head to the side and considered it for a moment.

"Sure."

He tried to smile but it didn't reach his eyes. I could see his shoulders had tensed up—they were practically around his ears.

"Come closer," I urged, and he shuffled over to me.

I grabbed the damp cloth and slowly began to slide it across his skin. I started on the side of his neck and ran it across his chest, which was smattered with a light forest of hairs, all the way over to his other shoulder. He leaned into the touch and followed it as I moved the cloth across his body.

I ran the material around in small circles on his skin, and felt his shoulders loosening and retreating from his ears under the firmness of my touch. I reached around and washed his upper back, then moved down to his lower back until I came around to...his belly.

I put the cloth aside and ran the back of my hand along the soft, sensitive skin of his stomach. I looked up at him, into those dark brown eyes of his. The tornadoes had gone, and all that remained were two big question marks.

"I think this could be my favorite part of your body," I said as I skimmed the light hairs that covered his belly.

"Uh, hello, have you seen my ass?" he asked, and I burst out laughing. He lifted his leg up, gave his ass a playful pat, and said, "'Cause this ass is something else."

"Agreed," I said as I leaned in for a sweet, satisfying kiss. I ran my hand up and down his meaty thigh, perilously close to the hole I had just pummelled with my cock, but far enough away so that he knew I was just teasing. "And for your information, yes, I have been with a big boy before."

"Oh," his eyes widened and his belly tightened. I couldn't tell if he was curious or jealous. Maybe both.

"Nothing serious," I said, continuing to stroke along his stomach. My eyes were transfixed by it. "He was a nice guy, but..." my voice trailed off.

I wanted to say *"he was nothing like you,"* but that wouldn't have been right or fair to anyone.

"But what?"

I looked up to see Nick clinging to my every word.

"Wait a minute," I said with a smile. "What happened to your *no talking* rule?"

"Right. Of course," he said, sitting fully upright. "Give me the best fuck of my life and *then* decide you don't want to talk. Typical male."

He folded his arms across his chest, but his burgeoning smile threatened his faux-serious demeanour.

"We can talk," I said as I picked up the damp cloth and continued gently rubbing along his front. "We can talk all night, if you like."

"That could be..." he looked around the room as if he were searching for the right words. Or maybe an escape route. "...nice."

"Great," I said, trying to contain the happiness that was bubbling inside of my chest. "I've worked up a bit of an appetite here. What do you say we share a pizza?"

"Share?" he scoffed. "Let's get one thing straight, Steel Crawford. Big boys don't share food. Especially not after ravenous sex like that."

"Duly noted," I said with a grin. "Best sex you ever had, huh?"

I kissed the top of his forehead and headed to the bedroom door. I was pretty sure I'd left my phone charging in the kitchen.

"I'll order the pizzas now."

"Do you mind if I have a shower?" Nick asked.

"No, go for it," I said. I could have sworn I heard him mutter something about cake, but I put it down to post-sex brain fog.

Thirty minutes later, the pizzas arrived just as Nick was coming out of the bathroom, wrapped in only a towel and drying off his shoulder-length hair.

"Holy shit," he said as he looked at the pizza boxes on the coffee table. All fourteen of them.

"I didn't know what you liked," I said, throwing my hands in the air.

"Ever thought of asking me?" he asked with a chuckle as he approached the tower of pizza boxes.

"Uh, you have literally been in the shower for half an hour," I said as I pulled him in close and kissed him again. I liked kissing him.

"Yeah, well, I like to be clean."

I picked up on a hint of defensiveness in his tone.

"What if I like you dirty?" I flashed him a cheeky grin.

"Wait, you're not into that, are you?"

"Huh? Into what?"

"Nevermind." Nick broke free of my grip, planted himself on the sofa, and peeled open the top pizza box. "Ooh, pepperoni."

His eyes lit up as he took the first bite.

I grabbed a slice of supreme and sat down next to him, watching him eat as he looked around the apartment.

"I like your place," he said in between mouthfuls. "It's got a nice view."

"Thanks. Yeah, it does. Although, I'll tell you something funny, when I bought the place I was actually afraid of heights."

He craned his neck and looked at me like I was a crazy person.

"If you're afraid of heights, then why did you buy a top-floor penthouse?"

It was a fair question.

"Because I didn't want to be afraid of heights. I thought, there's no better way of facing a fear than head on."

"And?" Nick asked, biting down on another slice. His eyes were glued to me.

"I still live here, don't I?"

He let out a chuckle and it was the sweetest sound I'd heard from him—in the last five minutes. My reply seemed to satisfy him and he wolfed down the remainder of the slice in two big bites.

When he was done, he looked over at me. There was a longing in his eyes, but nothing coming out of his lips.

"Come here," I said, patting the sofa next to me. "You like cuddles?"

"Do I!" His voice had the excitement of a child's as he lunged over to me, his towel falling from around his waist.

"Oh wait, you've got a little..." I reached for a napkin to wipe away some pizza that was glued to his cheek, but he winced away, as if in fright.

"Oh, sorry," he said when he saw that I was reaching for the napkin. "I thought you were going to do that thing where people lick their fingers and then wipe food off your face."

"Why would I do that?" I asked, puzzled.

"My grandma does it. I figured...don't worry about it."

He looked down at the floor.

I grabbed the napkin and then hooked his chin between my thumb and index finger as I gently lifted his face up.

"No wet fingers, I promise," I said as I wiped the small piece of food from his face. He shuffled as he sat, and for a moment it looked like he was squirming. "You okay?"

"Yeah, fine," he practically gulped the words.

From the corner of my eye, I could see his hands covering his growing erection.

"There, all done," I said as his face softened into a gentle smile. I eyed his naked body sprawled in front of me, his hardening cock pressed between his legs. "Are you cold? I can turn the heat up if you like."

"No." His voice rang out loudly as he nestled into my body in search of warmth. "Don't leave me."

"Okay, okay. I'm not going anywhere, Nick."

I reached around behind the sofa and grabbed the blanket that was there. I hurled it over our bodies and then patted it down to make sure he was completely covered. When I was certain that he was, I ran my hand up and down his back. A light shiver ran through his body, but after a few moments, he settled into stillness.

His head was on my chest and I could see him bobbing up and down with every breath I took. The gentle scent of my shampoo wafted into my nostrils. For some strange reason, it made me happy that he smelled like me.

"What would you like to do, baby?" I asked, wincing at the word *baby* escaping from my lips. Way too soon for that. Plus, he had made it clear this would be a one-time thing. A one-time, no-talking, sex-only thing.

But as he lay beside me, the warmth of our bodies radiating between us, my fingers playing with his wet hair, something stirred inside of me. Something that didn't want this to be a one-time-only thing.

It wasn't just the sex—though it had been absolutely incredible, mind-blowing sex. Our bodies fit so well together, as if they had been molded for each other. His softness, his curves, his muscles, his hard cock currently pressing into my leg—all of fit into place against my body so perfectly.

And it wasn't just the talking and the banter we had, or his ability to serve shit straight back to me, although I really loved that too. He was confident, not afraid to look me square in the eye and tell me exactly what he thought. That kind of raw, unfiltered honesty was beyond rare—it was practically non-existent in the modern dating world.

No, what was stirring in me was something deeper than that. It was a response to him and a need within me. The signs were subtle, almost indiscernible, but they were there nonetheless, hidden beneath the layers of physical pleasure and small talk.

The way his body had leaned into my touch when I'd cleaned him. The elation in his voice at the sight of the pizzas. The gleam of childish excitement in his eyes at the suggestion of cuddles. His fully rigid cock when I wiped his mouth...

I closed my eyes and tried to push the thoughts away. No. This wasn't the time to let myself start going down that path.

I tried to turn my head to look at him, but with the way he was lying on my chest, there was no way I could see his face. He hadn't answered my question. I was about to ask again, but as I opened my mouth, a deep breath escaped his lips. I listened carefully and could feel his heavy breathing as he drifted off to sleep. I ran my fingers lightly across the ridge of his shoulder.

This might be the only night I'd ever get with Nick. As much as I wanted it to last forever, I knew that it wouldn't. So there was no point in getting my hopes up or even beginning to think about what else could have been between us.

I just wanted to enjoy it all. To enjoy him. The heat of his body glued to my side, his head pressed into my chest, his legs wrapped up in mine.

This might be the only night I'd ever get to fall asleep with Nick Macklin in my arms on my sofa—and I was going to savor every single second of it.

CHAPTER SEVEN

NICK

"I can't believe it's been a week since you had sex with Steel and this is the first time we're catching up," Mikey's voice rang out excitedly.

I tore my eyes off my reflection in the mirror and looked over at him. He was getting ready too, adjusting the tiny apron around his waist until it was just right. But I could tell his mind was elsewhere. On my sex life, to be exact.

"I know. I'm sorry I haven't been around lately," I said apologetically. "I've just been working, working, working."

Mikey chuckled. "Yeah, working your ass around Steel's cock."

"Mikey Harrison, since when do you talk like—"

"You?" The cheeky little devil interrupted, but I couldn't help but smile.

"Hey, just because you're getting some good Daddy dick, don't get all attitude-y with me, please. I've got plenty of 'tude for the both of us," I said with a finger wag.

His laugh filled the air as he gave me a quick squeeze on the shoulders. "I could never take your place, Nick Macklin. You truly are one of a kind."

"Here," I said, holding out the bottle of lotion toward him. "Do my ass."

"Ah, just like old times," Mikey said with only the faintest hint of sarcasm as he grabbed the lotion from me.

Normally my caramel-toned skin didn't need any bronzer, but I had been working my ass off lately, so I could do with a little glow up. It was scary, but I'd become almost as pale as...Mikey. A frightening thought indeed.

"Are you looking after yourself though?" he asked as he spread the lotion across my lower back and over my cheeks, rubbing it into my skin in circular motions.

I sighed. "I guess."

The truth was, I wasn't really. I'd even lost five pounds, which was not a good thing to happen to a big boy. But I just literally didn't have time to eat some days. Between getting up at the crack of dawn to open the bakery, working there until the early afternoon, going home to have a quick nap, and then either working at The Tank Top or as a naked butler until midnight, looking after myself had taken a backseat.

"Hmph," Mikey exhaled and I knew he wasn't buying it.

"Hey, I gotta make the Benjamins, baby," I said, trying to lighten the mood.

"All done," Mikey said as he gave my ass a playful slap. "Oh and also—*Benjamins?*— we're not in a mid-'90s R&B music video, so there's no need for that sort of language."

"Mikey boy," I exclaimed. I was loving his newfound confidence, even if it meant he was serving it up to me.

Being with Stirling was clearly good for him. It wasn't just about being with someone good, though, it was about being with someone who allowed him to be his true self. Mikey had always had it in him, he'd just needed the right man to bring it out.

"You guys decent?" Hunter asked as he knocked on the door, only taking a half step in.

"No, but we're dressed," Mikey stole the words right out of my mouth.

"Look at you go, Mikey boy," I said as Hunter stepped into our makeshift changing room. "Ever since he's been bouncing on that Daddy dick," I said, turning to Hunter, "he's become a completely new boy."

"Hey," Mikey protested.

I raised my hand in the air. "I ain't mad at ya—"

"Stop talking like we're in the mid-'90s." He shot me a faux-pointed glare.

"Just be careful with all of that bouncing, that's all I'm saying. It might be fine for you, Mikey, but think about your Daddy." I lowered my voice for dramatic effect. "I heard that once guys hit forty, they need to start looking after their hips and shit."

"As someone who has forty in his rearview mirror, I can assure you that is incorrect," Hunter said with a smile, approaching me and tapping a white envelope against my chest.

"Ow," I said, raising my arms across my chest defensively. "Paper cuts. I have very sensitive skin, I'll have you know, Hunter Greyson."

Hunter scoffed but didn't bite. He knew me well enough by now to know when I was just ribbing him.

"Well, hopefully your sensitive skin doesn't have any issues with the big tip that's inside this envelope that Mr. Dobson left you after his party last week."

"Ooh," my eyes lit up like fairy lights and I rubbed my hands in glee. "Thank you," I said, turning to face him. "I really appreciate this, Hunter."

I'd been funneling all my money into the bakery, which, despite my regular orders for ornate, multi-tiered cakes, still couldn't manage to break even, let alone turn a profit. But I had spotted a cute pair of shorts in a bargain basement bin that were practically begging me to wear them. Luckily, I had the kind of body that could turn a pair of ten dollar shorts into an iconic fashion statement.

"You are more than welcome, Nick," Hunter said as he gave me a warm pat on the back. "You're one of the hardest-working people I've ever met. And I've worked in porn, so that's really saying something."

"Wait, you worked in porn?" Mikey asked as we both looked at each other.

"As what?" I asked Hunter.

"That, my boys, is a story for another time. And on that note, I'll see you out front in ten?" With a quick wave and mischievous smile, he was gone.

"Well, there you go," I said, looking around for my shoes. "You learn something new every day."

I grabbed them out of my duffle bag and started to put them on.

"And what about you, Mikey boy? How often are you working these days? We hardly ever work together anymore."

"Uh, yeah..." Mikey seemed more interested in tying his laces than looking at me.

"Mikey."

"I'm...working less." He looked up and I could see the discomfort written all across his face.

"Yeah, why's that?" I asked, narrowing my eyes at him.

"Well," His cheeks flushed with a rosy-pink blush. "I'm applying for college. Again. Well, actually, I'm applying again-again."

"Again-again, huh?"

"I'm basically trying to set the world record to see how many times a person can fail at applying for college."

"Ah, I see," I said. "Well, I think you're amazing. You're not a quitter, Mikey. Just keep trying, keep working, stay focused, and you'll get there. Those Daylesford tots will be lucky to have you as their childcare worker."

"Uh, yeah, about that. I've actually changed the course I am applying for."

"Oh."

"Yeah. I'm applying for...nursing. I know it's harder. Much harder. But with everything that's happening with Ma, and her deteriorating health, it just feels like the right choice. I want to do something that really helps people, you know?"

"Well, I couldn't be more proud of you," I said, giving my best friend a tight hug. "You'll get there, Mikey, I know you will."

"I'm not sure how Stirling feels about me doing, you know, this kind of work," he said, gesturing to his barely-there apron.

"Has he said anything?" I asked.

"No, not in so many words, but I guess it is something I have to think about."

"Fair enough." I nodded. While I could see his point, taking into consideration how his Daddy felt about his job was a considerate thing for him to be doing, a tiny part of me couldn't help but feel a little jealous.

Don't get me wrong, I was a hard worker and proud to be financially independent. But it would have been nice to know that I had someone in my life to rely on, even if it was just as a backup. I quickly pushed that ugly feeling down.

"So anyways, stop holding out on me," Mikey said with his bright blue eyes blinking excitedly at me. "Tell me everything about you and Steel. Is it Insta-official, yet?"

"What? No!" I said, flapping my arms in the air dismissively. "No, no, no. The only thing that it is—*officially*—is a one-time-only thing."

"Oh," Mikey said dejectedly.

To avoid the guilt vibes I knew would be coming my way, I turned and did a final check in the mirror. My hair was brushed and tied back in a neat ponytail, my face was freshly shaven, my belly, despite losing a few pounds, was shining like the sun, and my ass...well, every day was a good ass day for me. I smiled and gave a firm nod of approval to my reflection in the mirror.

"So, what is it, then?" Mikey asked as he stepped into view in the mirror behind me. "With you and Steel. I mean, you had sex with him, so you must like him a little."

"Mikey," I said, looking at myself and trying to ignore him in the reflection. "I had sex with him because I was horny. I still don't fully like the guy."

"But you've sorted stuff out?" The hopeful tone in his voice was mildly irritating. "I mean, you thought he was a massive jerk before. You don't think that anymore, right? And you had sex at his place and then stayed the night, so it wasn't just sex."

"Wait, how did you know I stayed the night?" I said, locking in on him in the mirror.

Mikey shrugged. "Daddies talk too, you know."

Hmm. I pursed my lips into an unimpressed pout. It wasn't a good look for me.

"But you like him a little bit more than before?"

Geez, Mikey really wasn't giving up on this.

"No," I replied defiantly.

I turned away from the mirror, not liking any of the faces I was making. The truth was, yes. Yes, I liked Steel...a little.

Well, maybe a bit more than just a little.

But I didn't want to get into it with Mikey right now. I didn't even want to be thinking about it myself.

How it had warmed my chest when I walked out of his shower and saw that he had ordered every single type of pizza for me. How good it had felt when he looked after me, whether it was wiping my mouth or covering me in a warm blanket. And how unbelievably nice it was to fall asleep with him on his sofa, our bodies pressed into each other in the most blissful way for the whole night.

But I still wasn't entirely sure about him. Sure, he wasn't the totally massive jerk I'd thought he was, but there were still other things I didn't like about him. Things that I hadn't told him, that maybe I should have. He may not have been a complete asshole, but he also wasn't the perfect saint that Mikey wanted me to believe that he was.

So there was that, but there was also...the *other* thing. The thing that had me jumping all over the internet whenever a random thought flew into my head, desperately looking for answers. It was the same thing that got my cock rock hard and dripping wet when Steel had wiped my mouth.

That thing? Yeah, I wasn't anywhere near ready to even go there.

Mikey turned and followed me as I walked across the room to grab my body spray. It was the final touch I always added before I was ready to get my naked butlering on.

Suddenly, all of the things I had going on in my life pummeled into my chest. I really didn't want to admit it to anyone—especially Mikey who was finally in a happy place in his life—but it was all starting to get to be too much for me.

I was working too much. I was stressing about money too much. I wasn't eating enough. And on top of all of that, I was starting to obsess over Steel...way too much.

I began spritzing myself and as the sweet, flowery smells that I loved so much absorbed their way into my pores, I closed my eyes and imagined a different life. One where I didn't have to constantly be worried about money and looking after my grandparents. One where I was able to ask for help and actually had a Daddy who looked after me.

A life that was fair.

"Where's Stirling tonight?" I asked once I was done spritzing myself into oblivion.

"He's hanging out with his friends."

"Will Steel be there?" I asked, even though I knew the answer.

Mikey nodded. "Yeah, probably."

"Figures," I said as I motioned for Mikey to join me and head out to the party. "I thought I could feel my ears burning."

CHAPTER EIGHT

STEEL

Three sets of interlaced fingers, with elbows teetered on the edge of a very small round table.

Three chins resting on said interlaced fingers.

Three pairs of eyes with their gaze firmly focused on...me.

"What?" I said, bringing the glass to my lips, knowing the cover would be futile.

"You know exactly what, Steel Crawford," Porter said, his face alight and his hefty torso practically bursting out of his corduroy navy jacket. Very un-Dom-like behavior from the man, but I let it slide. He took his jacket off as he kept his eyes glued to me.

They all did. Stirling and Hudson were just as bad. Like children in a schoolyard, waiting for their latest gossip fix. Hardly Daddy-like behavior from either one of them. But again, I let it slide.

"Guys, come on," Hudson finally said, peeling his eyes off me. Clearly the good guy within him had reactivated and he became, as always, the quad squad's voice of reason. "If Steel doesn't want to talk, he doesn't have to talk."

"Amen to that," I said, raising my glass in his direction with a relieved smile.

"But if he does want to talk to his lifelong best friends who he's known for over twenty years and who have seen him through all of the major ups and downs in his life and have been there for all of them..." Porter stopped and wheezed in a massive breath before continuing, "...then we'd be more than happy to listen."

A self-satisfied smile broke out across his face as he settled back onto one of the high stools we were all sitting on. Or at least, he tried to.

"I fucking hate these uncomfortable metal stools," he grumbled.

"I think they're *in* at the moment," Stirling offered, but was rebuked with a petulant look from Porter.

"Yeah, well they can fuck right *out* as far as I'm concerned. I need back support."

"Okay, grandpa," Hudson said, chuckling into his drink loudly enough to elicit snickers from Stirling and me.

"Hey," Porter said, lifting a finger to Hudson. "I haven't even started on you yet."

"What?" Hudson's eyes widened in innocence, as they always did whenever he thought he was getting in trouble.

It was almost cute, I guess. Although, cute was a weird word to use for the guy who carried a massive, burly facade of hard muscles and bright ink. In reality he was the least scary dude ever, not that you'd know it by looking at him. It came in handy on occasion.

"Oh look, there's Liam 'I'm Always Right' Wright," Porter shot back.

"Where?" Hudson's head spun around the bar so quickly he would have given Nick a run for his money if head snapping were a competitive sport.

"We'll deal with that later," Porter said as an incorrigible smirk settled on his lips. "But first, guys, we need to find a better place to hang out. This place is the pits."

"Uh, it literally is," I jumped in. You had to with these guys or you'd permanently be on the sidelines just watching the circus play out in front of you. "It's actually called The Hairy Armpit."

"Eww, are you fucking serious? Who chose this place?" Porter huffed.

Hudson raised his hand slowly, guiltily.

"Shit name. Too many drunk young people. Smells like...I want to say..." Porter stuck his nose out and sniffed the air in front of him, "...my creepy uncle Tom's musty basement. And. No. Back. Support. Hudson, you are officially off bar-picking duty, my friend."

We let out a chorus of sighs and nods.

Ever since The Laird had become a no-go zone—I mean, there was no way in hell any one of us would set foot in the place after we learned that it was owned by Mikey's dickass ex-boyfriend, especially after what the guy had tried to do to him—we'd been trying to find a new hangout.

It was proving to be quite the challenge. The Laird had been like our second home for the better part of a decade. We were having the Goldilocks problem with all the new places we went to. The places were either too big, too loud, and just too much. Or they were too small, too cramped with young people, and offered too little back support. There was nothing that was just right.

"Maybe one of us should open a bar," I joked.

The guys smiled, although Hudson's eyes kept darting around the bar, looking for something. Someone? I hadn't quite caught what Porter had said to him before about some Liam guy.

"At least we'd be able to run it properly," Porter said, the irritation slowly starting to leave his voice. "Anyway," he continued, now locking his eyes onto me like a stealth bomber acquiring and locking in its next target. "What would you like to tell us about your wild sexual adventures with a certain big boy you've been crushing on ever since your fortieth?"

"I have not been crushing on him since my fortieth," I sighed. "Okay, maybe I have. Just a little."

It wasn't worth even denying, I had been clear as day about my feelings for Nick with the guys.

"Kind of a lot," Stirling added, completely unnecessarily.

I wanted to shoot him a *gimme a break* look, but his green eyes were too warm and friendly. Besides, I knew there wasn't any malice behind his words.

"Well," I began slowly, not completely sure how I would sum up the events of the past week. "I met him at The Tank Top when I was out with Stirling and Mikey, and we got to talking."

"He didn't run away?" Hudson asked, his eyebrows raised in surprise.

"No," I said with a firm smile. "I booked a private dance with him."

"So I'm hearing that you...held him captive?" Porter teased.

"He was free to leave at any time," I shot back.

"I'm just kidding, geez," Porter said with a wink. "Go on, go on."

"Look, long story short, there was a bit of a misunderstanding. He thought he heard, no wait, he *did* overhear me saying something insensitive and completely stupid at Hudson's fortieth on the yacht. It was a thoughtless turn of phrase. But we talked about it and cleared things up."

"Yeah, he cleared things up with his cock," Stirling joked. Nick must've been rubbing off on Mikey, who was rubbing off on Stirling, who was now rubbing it in my face.

I may have confided a few of the finer details of my evening with Nick to him the next day. He was my best friend, after all. This time, though, I didn't care how friendly his eyes were. I flipped him the bird.

"Wait, you had sex with him?" Porter asked, slamming both of his hands onto the small table and sending our drinks jiggling and almost spilling over the edge of the glasses. His mouth was so wide open it was taking all of my self control not to throw a peanut into it.

"I did," I said, looking into the bottom of my drink.

But it hadn't been just sex—at least, not for me. Not that I was ready to say that part out loud yet, even to my closest friends.

"Have you been in touch since?" Hudson asked.

"Just a few texts back and forth, nothing much," I said. I could feel a nervous twitch rising from my stomach and lodging in my chest. What Nick and I had was barely anything. It was so fragile, and every time I was reminded of that, it made me feel uncertain. Worried. Just generally shitty

"He works like crazy."

The guys, sensing my discomfort, were about to move the conversation on when a very young and very drunk guy stumbled and fell across Hudson's back, pushing Hudson forward onto the table and almost spilling all of our drinks onto the floor.

"Whoa, sorry, man," the drunk guy's friend said as a look of fear gripped his face. Hudson got up, brushed himself off, and turned around to face them. "He's had too much to drink. I'm taking him home. Please don't hurt me."

"Get out," Hudson growled, and the guy's face turned an even paler shade of white.

"We're going, we're going." The guy dragged his friend to the front door. "I'm sorry," he yelled over his shoulder.

Stirling shook his head. "You shouldn't have scared the poor guy like that. He was terrified."

"He was only terrified because he assumed I was going to kick his ass."

"Uh, yeah, have you looked in the mirror lately?" Porter asked.

Hudson mumbled something into his glass before raising it and finishing the rest of his drink with one fell swoop.

"This place does suck," I said as I looked around at it properly for the first time. It wasn't offensively bad, but it was packed with a much younger clientele than The Laird attracted. "When did young people start looking so young?" I wondered out loud.

"Maybe when we started looking old?" Porter quipped. "Anyway, it's time for more drinks. Hudson, Mr. Tough and Scary Guy, be a dear and get us another round."

Hudson grimaced at Porter, while Porter batted his eyelids back at him, ever so sweetly.

"But I got the last round," Hudson grumbled.

"Trust me," Porter said leaning in. "You want to get this one."

He tilted his head, completely indiscreetly, in the direction of the bar. Hudson turned to check what Porter was pointing at and the color drained from his face, sending it deep into shit-scared pale white territory.

"What are you guys talking about?" Stirling asked, joining me in my complete confusion.

"Yeah, I feel like we've missed something, guys. Care to fill us in?" I added.

"Do you want to tell them or should I?" Porter asked Hudson.

The giant man grumbled again, but didn't say anything—at least, not anything intelligible.

"Fine. I'll tell them. You're not the only one with a crush, Steel," Porter began. "Hudson here has a massive crush on Liam "I'm always right" Wright."

"Why does that name ring a bell?" I asked.

"He's the weather dude on channel KDR-9," Porter said. I scrunched up my face, trying to recall the guy. "You know, the hot dude with the massive ass who always wears the tight pants that show off said ass."

"Oh yeah, now I'm with you," I said. "And he always turns so..."

"You can see his massive ass," Porter finished my thought for me.

I smiled as I remembered how the cute guy—with the disproportionately big behind—always made me stick around for the weather forecast at the end of the news, even though I could have just, you know, looked out the window and gotten a real-time weather forecast. I quickly stopped smiling when I saw the look Hudson was throwing at me. It sent a shiver down my spine. I could only imagine what that drunk guy's friend had felt.

"He doesn't just have a nice ass," Hudson said with a frown. "He's smart. He knows his shit. And he loves weather, he's truly passionate about it."

His frown disappeared, replaced by a wide, happy smile.

"Did you know there are three main kinds of clouds and that different types of clouds are named based on their shape and how high up they hover in the stratosphere? I learned that from him the other day."

Stirling, Porter, and I glanced around at each other, but Hudson was off and racing. As his closest friends, there was nothing else we could do...but watch.

"And sure, he has a nice butt, a *really* nice butt, but his smile is just so freaking adorable. He has dimples, you guys. Dimples. And I know that everybody goes on and on about his ass, but I actually think he's got some good shoulder definition happening too. I mean, he might need to come into the gym for some training, but I am sure I could develop a program for him."

Stirling opened his mouth to say something, but Porter tapped his forearm and frowned at him. Porter was clearly enjoying this too much.

"And he's funny, guys. Okay, okay, this is what he said the other day—'why did the cloud stay at home?'"

Silence.

"Oh, you actually want us to answer? Is that what we're doing?" Porter asked bitingly.

"Stop being a dick, Porter," I said, flicking his shoulder playfully with my hand. "Tell us, Hudson."

God, I hoped it wouldn't be as bad as I thought it was going to be.

"It was feeling under the weather," Hudson said, erupting into laughter, like it wasn't the worst joke we'd ever heard.

"Well then," Porter said, his lips parting mischievously. "All the more reason for you to go up to the bar, say hello, and introduce yourself to this amazing superstar of a weatherman."

"He does have a point," Stirling added. "If you want something, or someone, you have to go for it. I mean, look at me and Mikey. Nothing would have happened if I didn't take a chance, big guy."

"He's right, you know, Hudson. If you want it, you gotta go for it."

"Oh, hello," Porter said with a flash of drama as he looked at me. "Pot. Kettle. Black."

"What? We've moved on from me and we're talking about Hudson now," I explained to Porter.

"You guys are both in the same situation," Porter said, drumming his fingers on the table, making it shake. "You both need to stop making excuses. Hudson, if you like the guy, go say hello. And Steel, if Nick is always working, then go to his work and meet him where he is."

The four of us fell silent. A common occurrence after Porter spoke, but usually it was mainly out of shock at the oversharing of every single detail of his sex life.

"So..." Porter said, sitting up tall, a massive smile covering his face. "I've given you guys my patented three-point plan..."

Oh brother. We groaned in unison.

"Is he still going on about that?" Hudson asked, shaking his head.

"He doesn't forget a thing," Stirling reminded us, as if we needed it.

Porter continued, unperturbed, "And now this. Simple advice for my simple friends. You're welcome, guys. You. Are. Welcome."

After another round of groans, Hudson and Porter walked over to the bar to get some more drinks, avoiding the side of the bar where Liam and his friends were standing.

Porter's teasing words bounced around in my head. I would never admit it to the doofus, but he was right. If Nick was always working, maybe I should just pay him a visit at work. Though the idea of getting a private dance from him felt like it wasn't the right thing to do. It was almost redundant, especially after the incredible sex we'd had.

Stirling came over and sat beside me.

"You know," he said, smiling, "Nick's got a lot of jobs."

"I know that."

"He's a naked butler..."

I nodded.

"A go-go dancer at The Tank Top..."

More nodding.

"And he's also a clown and a...magician."

"Wait, what?" I studied Stirling's face to see if the guy was pulling my leg, but nope, he was serious.

"So, if you ever find yourself in dire need of a magician to come to your party of one, give Say The Magic Word a call."

"That's a real company?" I asked with a scoff.

"That's the company Nick works for, yes," Stirling replied, as cool and steady as always. A smile crossed his lips and crinkled around the edges of his green eyes.

"Give 'em a call, Steel, and, you know...just say the magic word."

CHAPTER NINE

NICK

There are two places where I do some of my best thinking: on the toilet and in the backseat of an Uber. And that's where I was right now—the backseat of an Uber, that is, on my way to a magician's gig. Although, right from the get go, I had a feeling something about this gig didn't quite add up. I mean, what sort of parents throw their kid a birthday at eight at night on a Wednesday?

But whatever, money was money. And the address boded well. It was the very definition of money. The apartments overlooking the bay were where the big spenders lived. So here I was, being driven across town...and thinking.

About Steel.

About the feeling of warmth that had flooded my insides when I got home each night over the past week and was greeted by a massive bouquet of red roses at my front door.

About having had the best sex of my life with the delectably gorgeous silver fox who made my insides go all gooey.

And about how I could never have sex with him again.

It was all one big, ginormous mistake.

And while I couldn't go back in time to fix it, I could make sure it would never happen again. I had to. I sighed as I rested my forehead against the cold car window. The buildings became larger and more imposing in the reflection, a sign that we were getting closer.

'Cause here's the thing, the thing I hadn't even told Mikey about because I didn't want to ruin the halo he seemed to think Steel had permanently wrapped around his head. And also because Steel was his boyfriend's best friend. I didn't want to do anything, or be that guy, that would be responsible for Mikey and Stirling's first fight.

See, I may have kinda, sorta...okay deffers, totally stalked Steel online. On Google. Wikipedia. Social media—well, except for LinkedIn because that's just gross. I even went through the archives of *The Daylesford Times*. The man had been featured there eight times.

And in all that searching, I learned something about him that was a total deal breaker for me.

Steel Crawford was not the self-made man he went around telling the world he was.

As it turned out, he was, in fact, a trust fund baby.

Look, I was twenty-four, actually almost twenty-five. I knew that life wasn't fair. If it were, my dad wouldn't have taken off before I was born, my mom wouldn't be in and out of rehab as often as I changed jeans, and I would've had a normal set of parents growing up.

But at the same time, I knew it could have been a million times worse. I didn't end up in the system, like so many other kids. I was taken in by two of the most incredible people in the world, my grandparents, and given the best start in life they could give me.

They weren't rich, far from it. They made an okay living from their bakery, but they had to make a lot of sacrifices and put in some serious hours to do it. I couldn't remember a single day when one of them wasn't working, and they'd been like that, every day, for the last forty-five years.

Seeing that growing up, it was no surprise that I had the discipline and work ethic that I did. I worked hard for my money. Maybe not everyone thought that the work I did was so great, but I wasn't ashamed of it.

I'd never had to rely on handouts or pity from anyone. Everything that I had—and sure, it may not have been much—was mine. I bought it with my money. I may have been renting a shoebox apartment that was the size of Steel's kitchen, but at least I was doing it on my own.

Not with some trust fund that had just landed in my lap when I turned twenty-one. A trust fund that allowed me to go to college debt-free (I'm assuming), become a lawyer and start my own law firm at the age of thirty-two (thanks, *The Daylesford Times*), and buy a penthouse in one of the swankiest buildings in the nicest part of Daylesford (thanks, Wikipedia).

A swanky building that the driver had just pulled up to. My brows pinched together tightly as I looked up at the towering building, lit up in a golden hue, and asked the driver, "Is this the right place?"

He turned around to look at me. "It is. You asked for 408 East Parkwood Avenue. Is there a problem?"

Yes, there was a problem. One huge, motherfucking, entitled, arrogant, privileged, trust fund baby of a problem.

"Nope, all good. Thanks," I said, forcing a quick smile.

I grabbed my bag and stepped out of the car. The cool night air hit my face. I dropped my bag to the ground and buttoned my jacket up, debating what I should do next.

Should I go back home or...should I go up?

I was pissed that he'd done this. His little trick might have been a cute experiment for him, but it was going to cost me a night of earnings. With a huff, I picked up my bag and walked through the spinning glass doors.

A fiery heat pooled in my belly during the long elevator ride up to his penthouse. Maybe I should have turned around and left the second I pulled up, but I didn't want to leave without giving him a piece of my mind. Good thing for me, I had jacked off that afternoon, so I knew I was thinking with my right head.

By the time the elevator dinged and the doors opened, my hands had become enraged fists stuck to the sides of my body.

And there he was. Standing ever so casually, his head tilted slightly and a carefree smile stretching his lips. He was dressed simply, in a pair of faded jeans and a white t-shirt. The materials clung to his biceps and his legs in a way that should have been outlawed.

He pulled his arms out from behind his back, revealing another bouquet of roses and a box of chocolates. He reached his arms out as I stepped out of the elevator and slowly walked toward him. My face blank. My lips tight. My jaw clenched.

"Well, hello there." His voice was deep, warm, and syrupy.

"Hey," I said, dropping my bag to the floor. It would make it easier to put my hand on my hip and give him my *unimpressed look and stance* combo.

"These are for you," he said as he closed the distance between us.

"Is this meant to be cute?" I said as I took the flowers and chocolates from him and dropped them onto the floor.

His expression changed, overtaken by a look of bemused shock which disappeared almost as soon as I had noticed it.

"Uh, yeah, I mean, I don't know...is it?" The faintest hint of a hopeful smile curled around the edges of his mouth. "Do you think I'm cute?"

He stepped in even closer and traced his finger along my shoulder, sending a gooey warmth throughout my entire body.

I stepped back. "I—I don't know. I mean, no. No, it's not cute, Steel. What are you playing at here?"

"Oh, I don't know," he said, sounding innocent. He wasn't innocent at all. The man knew damn well what he was doing. "I heard you're a magician..." He was acting all shy and coy.

"Yeah...so?"

Hand on hip. Cocky head tilt. Pouty lips. How was he going to talk his way out of this one?

"Well...I like magic tricks, Nick. Maybe you could show me a trick?"

More cute coyness.

"What are you even talking about, Steel? What kind of magic trick do you want?"

That was my mistake. I had engaged. I'd asked him a question. I could feel the power dynamic shift. The dark wooden floor turned into golden quicksand and I was being dragged down, straight into it.

"Well, maybe you can find a way to make my cock disappear down your..."

"Whoa," I said, raising my hand in the air for dramatic effect. "Do not finish that sentence, Steel Crawford. We are not in some cheesy '70s porno. We are not doing this."

"Doing what?" He smiled and looked at me.

Dammit. He kept smiling and kept looking at me. My defenses were down. I had to do something to bring them back up again.

"You're costing me money."

Ah, money. The only dependable argument I had in my armory.

"Oh, I'll pay you," Steel said and it should have sounded all sorts of wrong and sleazy and arrogant, but for some reason it didn't.

I *hmpfed* as loudly as I could. "I am not a..."

"Sex worker?" Great, now he was reading my mind. I thought I was meant to be the one endowed with magical powers here. "I know that, come in."

He stepped aside and waved his arm toward his sofa.

The sofa we had eaten pizza on. The sofa we had slept together on, cradled in each other's arms, our bodies glued to one another until well after the sun had risen.

I deliberately avoided walking to the sofa and instead veered right and headed into his dimly lit, all-white kitchen. I had one last round of fire left. He followed behind me, his bare feet padding softly against the dark hardwood floor.

I took my time, taking it all in. The white marble countertop, all the expensive-looking European appliances, and then I turned my head to those incredible floor-to-ceiling windows and that breathtaking view out across the entire city.

"You're Brad Pitt," I said when I finally spoke, looking straight into his glimmering light blue eyes.

"Huh?" A wrinkle creased his otherwise perfectly smooth forehead.

"And I'm Shania Twain," I continued, tracing my finger along the pristine, cool, white marble countertop. "And this..." I waved my hand in the air dismissively "...don't impress me much. None of it, Steel. The flowers. This apartment. Your attempt at whatever this is tonight. It might work on other boys, but it doesn't work on me."

"Well firstly," Steel said as he placed both hands on the countertop across from me. All I could see was the way his arm muscles flexed, peeking out from underneath his white shirt. "You get extra bonus points for the '90s music reference. I'm impressed."

"Well, good. You—you should be." It would have sounded more cocky if I hadn't stammered.

Shoot.

Before I knew what was happening, Steel had somehow ended up right next to me. Again with the magic tricks.

"I want to fuck you again." His warm breath filled my ear. I shuffled my feet and cleared my throat. "I want to fuck you right here, on this countertop."

I opened my mouth to say something—what, I wasn't entirely sure—but I was met with a gentle grazing of Steel's tongue along my lower lip. I closed my eyes and leaned in toward him.

"But first," his tongue was replaced with a finger across both of my lips. "I need you to say the magic word."

I opened my eyes and fell into his. The silence sizzled between us like a piece of meat hitting a hot grill.

"Yes," I breathed, and he smiled widely.

"Yes what?"

Okay, now he was just playing.

"Yes, I want you to fuck me."

Hearing myself say those dirty words made my already rock-hard cock pulse in anticipation.

"Where do you want me to fuck you?" His lips pressed into mine before I could answer.

"Here," I moaned into his lips. "Fuck me here. Fuck me here right now."

Dammit, why had I thought that jacking off once would work? Rookie mistake. I should have taken the day off and spent the time getting off until I had totally drained my balls. Maybe then I would have been strong enough not to succumb to his silver fox superpowers.

Maybe.

Continuing his magician-like wizardry, he produced condoms and lube seemingly out of nowhere. Not to be outdone, I made my clothes fall off my body pretty damn quick too. His breath caught in his throat as he took me in, dragging his lust-filled eyes up and down the length of my exquisite, full-figured body.

"God, you're so beautiful." His voice had turned low and raspy. He stepped in toward me and greeted my lips with the gentlest of kisses. He ran his tongue along my lower lip, slowly, as if he were savoring the taste.

I pushed him back and our eyes locked. "Take it off," I said, gesturing at his shirt. He obeyed and his muscular frame looked heavenly, silhouetted against the dim kitchen lighting. He was beautiful too, but I wasn't going to tell him that. At least, not yet.

He brought his lips back to mine as I felt his hands gripping the sides of my belly before traveling lower onto my hips. With a steady strength, he lifted me up onto the white marble countertop. I couldn't tell if I was more turned on at the show of slow strength he was teasing me with, or the fact that he managed to raise me so effortlessly. Probably both.

The next thing I knew, I had the cold, hard countertop pressed against my back and the warmth of Steel's body on top of me. He reached around and pressed a lubed-up finger against me before sliding it in. Slowly, again, like he had all the time in the world.

He opened me up with another finger, followed by one more. I was hungry for him now, famished, actually. He pulled away and slipped a condom on, while I stared at the ceiling and took a breath.

What the hell was I doing? Fuck it. It felt good, so I was going to go with it.

I closed my eyes as he entered me, the heat and friction building inside of me as my body took every last inch of him. His heavy balls landed against my skin. My eyes flew open as I threw my head back and hissed out, "Yesssss."

He felt so good inside of me. It didn't have the urgency and the desperate need of the first time we were together. It was slower. We were looking into each other's eyes and silently working together with the rhythm of our bodies, gradually building and rising, as we rode the same wave of pleasure.

"I want you to come," Steel said after what felt like an eternity, as he continued thrusting deep into me. He wrapped his fingers into a tight fist around my cock. "I want to see your beautiful face as I make you come. I want to see your eyes roll into the back of your head. I want to hear all the sounds that you make. I want all of you, Nick."

"Okay."

I thought I said it out loud. I wasn't sure. The surges of pleasure pulsing through my body were unlike anything I had ever felt before. How was he doing this to me?

I wrapped my hands around his neck to steady myself. My eyes on his, his hand on my cock, furiously jerking it tighter and harder. A few more strokes and then...the sweet surrender of release.

I tilted my head back and moaned as I felt the sticky ropes of my release spraying over my chest and belly. When I looked up at Steel again, his eyes were still on me, darting across my face, as if he was committing it to memory.

His jaw clenched and I looked down to see his arm muscles twitching furiously. A few moments later, his whole face contorted and he let out a deep, guttural groan as his release joined mine. The scent of our salty flavors and sweaty bodies combined and filled the air around us. It was...intoxicating.

He brushed a finger across my cheek and peppered me with gentle kisses along my sweat-drenched forehead. The cold marble surface under me had transformed into a soft cloud and he and I were floating weightlessly through time and space.

I had walked into Steel's apartment wanting to give him a piece of my mind. Instead, I gave him a piece of my ass, and maybe even a little, tiny, eensy-weensy piece of my heart.

That terrified me. But at the same time, it didn't feel like the worst thing in the world, either.

CHAPTER TEN

STEEL

"Remind us again why we're here?" I asked Porter.

Hudson had just arrived and was finishing up giving everyone a round of bear hugs, while Stirling and Mikey looked about as nervous as you'd expect two people who had never been to a BDSM club before to look.

"What?" Porter widened his eyes at me. "I wanted someplace that was low-key and discreet."

"So, a BDSM club, then?" Stirling asked, his voice cracking uncharacteristically.

The big man looked around the place nervously, while Mikey clung to him like he was hanging on for dear life. Every once in a while, Mikey's eyes would dart around the place as well, shooting furtive glances at the surroundings.

"Hey, it's guaranteed privacy. You know how they are here," Porter said, looking in Hudson's direction for backup.

"That is true," Hudson agreed with a nod. "What happens at Revolver, stays at Revolver."

"And you know..." Porter continued, "...being the mayor's chief of staff means that I'm highly visible, which means that I need to be incredibly careful. But it doesn't mean that I'm not allowed to have a little fun on my fortieth birthday."

His face lit up as he looked around the place. This was pretty much the man's second home. Mine too, truth be told. Or at least, it used to be. I hadn't felt like coming here as often over the last few months. It just didn't give me the same rush that it used to.

"Besides, that whole *naked butler for your fortieth birthday party* thing is so six months ago. No offense, Mikey."

"None taken," Mikey replied with a smile, and for the first time, his white-knuckle grip around Stirling's waist loosened a little. "Just like it's not offensive to call you the Samantha of the group, right?"

Porter groaned, but smiled. "Are these guys still doing that?"

Mikey nodded. "But it's so funny. I mean, not only are you a total sl—I mean, you have a healthy sex drive like she does—but you have the same surname as well. Jones."

Hudson, Stirling, and I all looked at each other as if we'd just discovered blowjobs for the first time.

"How did we not figure this out before, guys?" Hudson finally asked.

Stirling and I shrugged.

"Do you want to know something else that will totally blow your minds?" Porter asked mischievously.

"I don't know, do we?" I asked, looking around at the other guys.

"My middle name is Sam. Well, Samuel, actually. Porter Samuel Jones. But same-difference."

"Oh my god, how can that be?" Stirling asked.

"Don't know," Porter said smiling. "I was born a few years before the show, so it's really just a coincidence."

"But what a fucking coincidence," I said.

"That's insane," Hudson chimed in. After a few moments of putting our minds back together, I broke the silence. "Well, since we do have some newcomers here with us tonight," I said. "Why don't you give Stirling and Mikey a little rundown of this place and how it works, Porter?"

He agreed with a sharp nod. We were sitting at the bar in the main lounge area. Porter, not one to ever shy away from being the center of attention, got up and motioned for Hudson, Stirling, Mikey, and I to huddle in around him a little closer.

"Alright," he began, putting on a more formal voice as we gathered around. "Gentlemen, on behalf of all the kinksters here, I warmly welcome you to Dayleford's premier BDSM club, Revolver. And more importantly...to my fortieth birthday celebration!"

"Stirling, Mikey, get out while you can," I joked.

Ignoring me, Porter continued, "Our scheduled party time is from now until whenever the fuck we feel like wrapping up. We will shortly be moving to the blue room in the corner over there, where the VIP, invite-only party will take place."

"Somebody make him stop," Stirling grumbled, but with a smile. "He's like a creepy flight attendant. It's going to give me nightmares."

"I'll take care of you, Daddy," Mikey said, wrapping himself even closer around Stirling's body.

Thankfully, Hudson jumped in and took over explaining the layout of the club. It was really quite simple. We were in the main lounge and bar area, which as he pointed out, only served non-alcoholic drinks for obvious safety reasons. It was dimly lit, yet bright enough for everyone to see each other.

There were a number of seating options, including plush sofas in the middle of the space, a few leather booths along one wall, a couple of tables and chairs across the other wall, and stools along the main bar. It was early in the evening so there were only a few people around. Stirling and Mikey said nothing, just nodding as they looked around the lounge, taking it all in.

"Have you ever been to a BDSM club before, Mikey?" I asked. A flash of panic swept over his bright blue eyes. "It's okay if you haven't," I quickly added as I noticed Stirling rubbing his back gently. "It's not a scary place at all, I promise you."

"It isn't," Hudson said, flashing him a warm smile. "This lounge right here is a good place to come to if you want to just sit, chill, and talk. Not much 'stuff' happens here. This is more of a social space, or a quiet zone, if you need that."

"So, where does the stuff happen?" Mikey asked quietly, but with a steely determination underpinning his voice. He was clearly a little nervous, but pushing through it. Having his Daddy by his side helped.

"The club is divided into four main areas," Porter said. "Coming out of each corner of this lounge, there is a corridor that leads to a particular area. The owner is a great guy and he changes things up frequently. So there's a sign before you enter the space that will tell you exactly what that space is currently being used for. One night it might be used for rope and bondage kink, or it might be for a spanking scene..."

Stirling and Mikey glanced at each other and a flush of red crept up both of their necks.

"It all depends and it changes frequently, so my advice is to read the sign carefully so that you know what you're stepping into."

"See, over there," Porter continued, pointing his head at the corner with an open door and a blue neon light emanating from it. We all nodded. "That's where my party will be tonight. We'll head over there shortly. It's a private space so only people on the guest list will be able to enter. There's a bar and drink service in there as well, and it's a clothes-on kinda party."

He winked.

"Good to know," Stirling said as his shoulders started to loosen a little.

"The other corners, well, they all lead to areas where you'll find all sorts of people, wearing all sorts of outfits, exploring all sorts of things. You're all free to wander around the entire club tonight if you like, or you can stay in the blue room and lounge area. It's totally up to you guys and what you're in the mood for."

"Are you guys okay so far?" I said, looking over at Stirling and Mikey.

Coming to a BDSM club for the first time was a big deal. It was something you'd never forget, but unfortunately, people had a lot of incorrect ideas and sometimes even negative misconceptions about what actually happened at a place like Revolver.

They both nodded, and I could see that despite still being a little tentative, they were both becoming more comfortable with their surroundings.

"I think I'd just like to stay in the blue room tonight," Mikey said softly, looking up at his Daddy.

"That's perfectly fine with me, Mikey," Stirling said as he planted a kiss on his forehead.

"But maybe next time, we can explore a bit more?" Mikey looked up and was met with Stirling's mouth practically falling off his face.

We all chuckled at his reaction. There was no way of escaping it, Stirling was still finding his feet as a Daddy.

"Two more quick things," Porter said, drawing our attention again. "A reminder that the entire club is non-smoking, that includes lavatories and showers."

"Geez, make him stop," Hudson said.

"Hey, it's my birthday," Porter said. "So let me have this airline host fantasy, please."

"Is that what it was?" Mikey said with a grin. "I couldn't tell."

That earned him a round of laughs from the group. Porter took it all in his stride.

"Side note, Mikey," I said with a grin. "Don't ever fly with Porter. We've flown together like, what, five, six times over the years? And every time we've flown together, he's fucked a flight attendant."

Mikey's laugh filled the air.

"That is hilarious," he said.

I checked on Porter, who was preening with pride, so I knew he wasn't taking offense.

"That's nothing," Hudson said. "One time when we were flying together, Porter fucked the pilot...during the flight."

Everyone gasped as Porter gave Hudson the finger.

"There were three pilots on the flight, you guys. It was totally safe," he said with a satisfied smirk. "I can't help it if I have a high sex drive. It's not something that just goes away, even at thirty thousand feet, and I make no apologies for it. My libido wants what my libido wants."

"So are you finished with your airline host fantasy yet?" I asked, smiling.

"Just one more thing," he said as he looked at us with a more serious expression on his face. "I know that this is a BDSM club, but what it boils down to is that this place is about people, okay? Please treat everyone with respect, because that's what we're about here. Clear communication, no judgment, and always, always, always, ask for consent."

We all nodded, and with that, we got up and made our way into the blue room to begin Porter's fortieth birthday bash. As we walked across the lounge, I pulled up beside Mikey and Stirling.

"Are you guys really okay?" I asked in a low voice.

Stirling was my best friend and I wanted to make sure he was comfortable. And Mikey just looked so sweet and innocent, although given the question he'd stumped Stirling with before, maybe that was an assumption worth examining. Bottom line, I just wanted them both to feel good and safe here at Revolver.

"I think we are. Right, Mikey?" Stirling said with a nod and a glance over at his boy.

"Yeah, I am. It's not as scary as I thought it would be. It's almost...normal," Mikey said.

"Well, fancy that," I said jokingly. "We're not all constantly walking around wearing leather and flogging each other with whips."

The three of us laughed.

"We actually did invite Nick as well," I said, turning to Mikey. "Porter thought it would be nice for him to be here, seeing as he's your best friend and all."

"Yeah, *Porter* thought," Stirling said as he eyed me briefly.

I stiffened a little. He wasn't being subtle, but he wasn't completely wrong, either. I did want Nick here, and part of it was so that Mikey would feel more comfortable, but part of it was for me, too. Although, as I was quickly discovering about Nick Macklin, the boy ran hot and cold, and I was having a hard time keeping up with it.

One minute he was angry and all cocky with me. The next, I was inside of him and feeling so close and connected. Then I didn't hear from the guy for days, and only got short answers back when he did text. The boy was a mystery wrapped in a riddle.

But it didn't make me not want him. Far from it.

His teasing was tantalizing. It drew me in. It increased my burning hunger for him even more. He may not have been making it easy for me, but I was a self-made man, in business as well as in pleasure.

Sure, I may have had a better start in life than most. I was born into a wealthy family. Old money. But I took the silver spoon out of my mouth at a young age and worked hard for everything I had.

You can't buy good grades. You can't buy graduating at the top of your class. You can't buy the dedication, passion, commitment, and sacrifice you need to have to get your business off the ground and successful. I did it all, and I did it all on my own.

But it came at a price. Love. It was the only thing to have eluded me this long. As fulfilling as my work was, as much as I loved my friends and my community at the club, it didn't make up for the fact that I didn't have a special someone by my side.

A boy.

But not just any boy. I loved seeing what Stirling and Mikey had, it was truly beautiful, but that wasn't exactly the kind of Daddy/boy relationship I wanted. Yes, I wanted someone younger who I could look after and take care of. But I needed something more, too.

Fire.

Fearlessness.

A boy with zero filter who gave zero fucks.

And a round, soft, hairy belly was just an added bonus.

Someone who stood up to me and gave as good as he got. Up to a point, of course. The thought of disciplining the defiance out of a boy turned me on like nothing else.

The thought of that boy being Nick, well, that was enough to get me rock hard in record time.

Wanting to avoid a massive tent pole forming in my pants, I asked Mikey, "Have you spoken to him recently?"

"I have," Mikey said with an impish grin, followed by a heavy silence. He was probably enjoying this. He and Stirling probably both were.

"Did he say anything about...him coming over to my place last week?"

"He may have mentioned it, and he may have mentioned your corny magician joke, too."

I winced as a heavy chuckle erupted out of Stirling.

"Not my finest hour," I conceded.

Then silence again. Mikey had clearly been taking lessons from the king of silence—Stirling was notorious for not talking. But with him I knew how to pry out the information that I needed. He'd been my best friend for half of my life, so I knew which delicate levers to push and pull to get him to feel safe and open up. With Mikey, because I didn't know him well, not so much.

"Has he said anything about *me?*" I finally asked, deciding to bite the bullet and let the most pathetic words I had ever uttered spill out of me. Suddenly, a sweet scent filled my nostrils. It was delicate, strawberry-filled, and warmly inviting.

"I don't know," Mikey said as he turned to look at me. "Why don't you ask him yourself? He's standing right behind you."

I whipped my head around and there he was. Hands on hips, head tilted to the side, and blowing a big pink bubble out of his mouth. It popped as I took a step closer to him and he chewed loudly on it.

He was so fucking cocky.

He smelled like a field of strawberries.

His eyes made me melt.

The boy was going to be mine.

CHAPTER ELEVEN

NICK

This would be the part of the movie that would need a few close-ups.

Firstly, a zoomed-in shot of the casual terror that shot across Steel's face when he saw me standing there behind him. Was it wrong that it made me shiver in delight to see the silver fox Daddy looking so petrified and yet so sweetly adorable at the same time?

I knew...that he knew...that I heard...what he said.

It would have made me look like a total dick, but I came *this close* to rubbing my hands in glee at the deliciousness of my timing, pulling up at Revolver just as I did and hearing him ask my best friend that question.

Because the truth was, I hadn't really spoken to Mikey about Steel a lot. Which was a little unusual for us. We usually told each other everything, but there was something different about what was going on with Steel. I needed some time to figure this stuff out in my own head as well.

"Oh, hey, Nick," Steel said, and all of a sudden the sun rose in the sky, lighting up the darkened lounge.

Oh no, my mistake. Steel was just smiling. My breath hitched in my throat.

I guess that would be the cue for my close-up. But first, I would start with a wide shot, because my body was looking a thousand different sorts of gorgeous tonight. I was wearing all black. Not because black with slimming, far from it. This black clung to my curves like a rock climber to a cliff face.

My thick thighs, my huge round ass, my hefty belly, and my bulging biceps...all of it on display in its full, big glory for the world to see. And by the looks of it, Steel was very much enjoying the view right in front of him.

My view wasn't so bad, either.

Steel was dressed more like a rockstar than a lawyer. He had on dark navy jeans that sculpted around his tight ass nicely. He wore a faded gray Metallica shirt that rode up his arms, showing off his chiselled pecs and wide shoulders perfectly. He also had on a couple of leather wristbands and he wore his silver fox mane wet and messy.

Wet and messy—Ha, that would deffers be the theme for this evening.

"Hey, Steel," I said, trying my best to keep my cool. "Am I interrupting something?"

I batted my eyelids a few times and smiled as sweetly as I could.

"We'll leave you guys to it," Stirling interjected, before he and Mikey disappeared into thin air. In fact, as was always the case when I was standing in front of Steel, the whole world disappeared into thin air.

It was just him and me. Nothing else mattered. Nothing else even existed.

"It's good to see you," Steel said. His voice was steady and sincere.

"It is..." I wasn't sure if I was asking him a question or agreeing with the man.

The truth was, I had so many conflicting thoughts and emotions about Steel that it made it hard for me to figure out what I felt, because there was so much I still didn't know. About him—and about me too.

He wasn't making it easy for me.

On the one shoulder, he was dressed like the devil—a sexy devil, of course, in a leather harness and assless chaps that would look divine on Steel. Devil Steel was a jerk. Typical old-school money, the kind of asshole that thinks he can just buy everything...and everyone.

But on the other shoulder was angelic Steel, just wearing a simple white—*angelic*—jockstrap. This was the Steel that Mikey knew and liked and kept trying to convince me that maybe I should like, too. Angelic Steel looked after me, treated me well, and made me feel good. Sexy. Wanted.

The question I was struggling to answer was: which Steel was the real deal?

"Oh, so you decided to come after all?" he asked as I realized I had probably been making googly eyes at him for at least the last three minutes. His light blue eyes were soft around the edges. There was a genuine warmth behind them.

"No, I'm not here for the party. I have a scene here," I replied, needing to remind myself as much as tell him.

"Oh, what sort of scene?" There was curiosity in his tone, but no judgment at all.

"A sploshing demonstration," I said.

"That's wet and messy play, isn't it?"

"Very good," I replied with a smile. "Are you into it?"

"No," he said with a firm headshake. "But that's the beauty of a place like this. There's room for everyone, and it's safe to explore all sorts of kinks and desires."

Hmm...*all sorts?* Even the sorts that were surging through my mind, as if on loop, twenty-four-seven?

I wondered.

I hoped.

I imagined what it might feel like to tell him. *Might*.

"I should get going. I need to get set up," I said. I was surprised to hear so much reluctance in my own voice.

"Of course. I didn't mean to hold you up," Steel said, sounding way too formal.

"You're welcome to come and check it out. The demonstration, I mean. If you want to."

"I do," he said with an eager gleam in his eyes. "I definitely want to watch you. I'll see if I can make it out at some point."

"Right," I said, nodding as I started to head over to where I was meant to go. "Please say happy birthday to Porter from me."

I threw a playful smile over my shoulder.

"I will. I might see you later."

God, I hoped so. His voice sent a warm wave of desire through me.

It was my first time at Revolver. I'd heard a lot about this place, pretty much all of it good, and from my experience so far, I could see why it had such a good reputation.

All of the staff here, the members, everyone was just so friendly and nice and normal. I brought the cake in with me and immediately, I was shown around the place and made to feel super comfortable and relaxed.

It was my first time doing a demonstration in public, but since Mason, the owner of The Tank Top, was best friends with the owner of Revolver, it must have come up at some point between them, and what can I say? My reputation must have preceded me. Plus, the money would be amazing, so hell yeah, I was in.

I was settled, comfortable, and ready to do this.

I stepped onto the stage. The cake was already in position, under a spotlight, and at least four feet tall. I smiled. Grandma had done a great job. The audience was sitting on all four sides of the stage, they could choose their viewing position themselves. It was hard to see how many people were in the space, but it looked like maybe a dozen or so.

Music started playing in the background, something rhythmic and tropical-sounding, but not loud enough to be distracting. I was wearing a tight pair of black boxer briefs and nothing else. I wanted it to be simple.

A big cake, a big boy, and a big mess.

I strutted over to the cake, walking all the way around it, so that everyone in the room got a chance to feast on the delicacy that stood before them. That would be me—the cake was a supporting character. I peered into the audience one last time to see whether Steel had been able to make it, but I couldn't see him anywhere.

I took a breath and re-focused. Now was not the time to indulge in my silver fox fantasy. I was a professional and I had a show to put on for the people. And I wanted it to be good. No, wait, scratch that. I wanted it to be so fucking good that it became the scene that shows up in the movie trailer and makes people say, "I have to see that movie."

I wanted this demonstration to be iconic, like the water scene from *Flashdance*, or the J.Lo pole dance in *Hustlers*, or like Britney Spears jumping up and down on her bed and dancing to a Madonna song in *Crossroads*.

Now that is one seriously underrated film.

But back to me, the cake, and the erotic sitting demonstration. As I had explained to Tristan and Sam, it wasn't just about sitting on the cake. That was the culmination, the climax, if you will, but there was a whole lot of lead-up to it, as well. It was a process, a journey into wetness and messiness.

I scooped my hand across a tier of the cake, collecting a palmful of white icing. I lifted my hand into the air and then brought it down, rubbing it diagonally across my chest, down across my belly, and around to the side of my hip. It left a trail of sugary sweetness that glistened against my tan skin.

Next up was my trailer-stealing move. See, here's the thing. Most people think that plus-size people aren't flexible, to which I say, fuck that. I stepped a few feet away from the cake and did a sexy little shimmy. Then I started to bend my knees, and as I did, I leaned backward and outstretched my arm toward the cake.

I could hear gasps coming from the audience as I bent my knees lower and lower...until my back was parallel to the floor. With both hands, I grabbed some cake, held it over me and then squished it, letting the pieces crumble over my body. Yeah, that was the money shot right there.

Slowly, I brought my body back up into an upright position, walking around the cake to let everyone see just how messy I was getting.

And now it was time for the pièce de résistance. The actual cake-sitting part. This was always my favorite bit because it just felt so squishy and fun. It didn't really do anything for me sexually, but I hoped it did something for the people watching.

I approached the cake and then turned around. I could hear people in the audience getting up and moving, scrambling to get a better view of me. I leaned my butt out seductively and stepped back so that my calves were touching the bottom tier of the cake.

"Here I go, you guys," I said loudly enough for everyone to hear. When it came to the sitting part, I didn't mess around.

I did it in one steady sit.

The cake crumbled around my ass, my legs, and my back, as I sank down into it as if it were a comfortable lounge chair. The spongy firmness brushed against my skin, almost tickling me. I heard a few gasps and maybe even a moan or two at the sight of me lowering myself onto—and into—the cake.

As soon as I had fully sat down, I rolled over onto my hands and knees, and playfully grabbed at any pieces of the cake that were still untouched and rubbed them down my arms and over my body.

The rest of the demonstration went by until there was no cake left because almost every part of my body was covered in it. An attendant from the club came up when I nodded to him and wrapped me in a bathrobe.

I was told not to expect the audience to clap or cheer at the end of the demonstration, but as the attendant led me away, I heard whisper-shouts of, *"that was amazing,"* and *"thank you for sharing that."* It made me feel warm and fuzzy inside, while being all sugary and icing-frosty on the outside.

I was taken into a well-lit room that had an adjoining bathroom for me to get cleaned up in. The attendant pointed out coffee, tea, and water that was set out on the table, and then he left, locking the door behind him.

Not a moment later, there was a knock on the door. Maybe the attendant had forgotten something?

I opened the door and a fierce heat rocked my body. It was Steel.

"Hey, how are you?" he asked, and the gentleness in his voice soothed me instantly.

"I'm good," I said, motioning for him to come in and closing the door behind him as he stepped into the room.

"Did you watch the demonstration?" I asked.

"No." His face was long and apologetic. "I couldn't get away. I'm sorry, I wanted to. I really did. But Porter was being...Porter."

I believed him.

He had a way of talking that made me trust him. But there were other tones in his voice, too, tones that I didn't yet recognize. Tones that he hid behind and that filled my head with endless doubt and confusion.

"That's one hundred percent okay," I said as I walked over to the mirror and grabbed a tissue, starting to wipe off the little bits of cake that had made their way onto my face and neck. "You're here for your friend's birthday. I totally get that."

"But I want to be here for you," Steel said, closing the space between us. His woodsy cologne filled the air. It was strong and powerful, just like he was. "I couldn't be there for the demonstration, but, if you would like it, I'd love to be here for the aftercare."

"Aftercare?" I said, shooting him a puzzled look.

"Yeah, you know. The stuff that happens after a scene...or after sex."

"You mean like snuggles and pizza?" I asked, and he let out a hearty laugh.

"Well, yeah, I guess that's a type of aftercare. It's anything you do to look after someone with whom you've shared a beautiful..."

His fingers brushed against my flushed cheek.

"Wonderful..."

The same fingers trailed up along my neck.

"Best sex of your life..."

Now they were dragging through the back of my hair.

"Experience."

Our lips collided.

"God, now I know why I thought you tasted like cake the first time you came over to my place," Steel said, pulling away from me briefly.

I grabbed him by his shirt and pulled his face back to mine. I wasn't done kissing this sexy Daddy just yet. He indulged me for a few more moments before pulling away again, and saying, "I want to keep kissing you. Believe me, I do. But can I please help you get cleaned up first?"

Hearing those words, hearing this man say that he wanted to look after me in that way, sent a low moan tearing from deep in my chest. He had no idea just how much I wanted that. I nodded.

"I need words," he murmured.

"Yes," I said, clearing my throat.

I closed my eyes as I let a wave of bliss wash all over me.

Had I just found my perfect Daddy?

CHAPTER TWELVE

STEEL

Nick closed his eyes as the warm water fell over both of us. My skin had flushed with heat when he had said that word. It was the last word he had uttered before a silence fell between us.

Yes.

From then on, it had been head nods and gentle murmurs of agreement.

I suggested we jump into the shower as that would be the easiest way to wash all of the cake off his body. He nodded, his brown hair cascading around his shoulders.

I offered to peel off his black boxer briefs and he nodded and cooed at the same time. It was the sweetest sound I had ever heard.

As much as I loved the cocky heat he would gladly direct at me, seeing Nick like this, so soft and agreeable, made my heart do a series of backflips and somersaults. I felt like I was radiating pure euphoria.

There was so much I still didn't know about him. Like him not knowing what aftercare was. That was something new I had learnt about him tonight. Maybe his cockiness and attitude were a defense, and perhaps Nick Macklin was less experienced as a boy than I had previously thought.

He slowly opened his eyes as I began to brush my hands across his soft skin, wiping him cleaner with every caress. The black-tiled shower we were in brought out the caramel glow of his skin. His flesh, wet underneath my fingertips, was enticing, and it was difficult not to get hard.

But this wasn't about sex.

This was about him, and about me showing him that I could look after him. I knew we had gotten off to a bumpy start, so it was important for me to show him some stability, some strength. I wanted him to feel like he could trust me. Besides, I had a feeling he'd end up in my bed again by the end of the night.

I was beyond disappointed that I had missed most of Nick's demonstration. I'd walked in on what looked like the final few moments, because of course, Porter had demanded everyone's attention and I hadn't been able to slip away any sooner. Seeing as it was his fortieth birthday party, I let it slide this time.

I wasn't into sploshing myself, but sweet mercy, Nick knew how to work a room. I had seen countless demonstrations at the club before, but I had never felt that level of excitement from the audience. The air was positively crackling with intensity. And Nick looked sexy as fuck, down on his hands and knees and writhing around looking so...dirty.

I knelt down and spun Nick around. I slid my fingers down his lower back, down over his impressively full butt cheeks, and across his legs, cleaning him up with every stroke as the water made its way down his back, leaving glistening droplets across his skin.

Of course, while I was on my knees, and at eye level with his gorgeous ass, I couldn't help but take it all in. It was so full, so round, and just slightly hairy. It was a thing of beauty and a source of so much pleasure.

"I need to make sure you're thoroughly clean, Nick. Everywhere," I said, looking up at him.

I could see his head nodding vigorously as he lifted one leg up, grabbing it by the knee, and gently parted his cheeks with his other hand.

His glistening, wet, pink hole was so inviting. I leaned in and dragged my tongue across its sensitive surface. Nick's entire body trembled and for a moment, I thought he would lose his balance and slip. I wrapped my hands around his hips to steady him before launching into a light tongue teasing.

The steam from the shower was making it foggy and a little hard to see down at butt-level, but his moans of pleasure were all the guidance I needed. Was there anything tastier than eating out the delicious hole of a boy that ignited your insides and made you feel more alive than you could ever remember feeling? Especially when said hole carried the sweetest aftertaste of cake. I mean, ass and cake—how could you go wrong with that?

My tongue wasn't just teasing Nick, though. I was now hard as a rock, too. The groans coming out of the boy's mouth were getting hungrier, needier.

I stood back up and breathed into his ear, "Wanna come back to my place?"

He turned around, his eyes ablaze with a desperate lust that made me want to take him right there and then. But the responsible Daddy side of me knew that wouldn't be appropriate.

"Yes," Nick said, before adding, "right now."

Thirty minutes later we were back at my place and Nick was lying naked on my bed. He placed his hands on the back of his thighs and pulled his knees up to his chest, knowing how much the sight drove me crazy. A red-hot heat flew through me as his chocolate-brown eyes looked up at me, round and blinking intently. His chest was heaving wildly. He was so exposed. So vulnerable. So ready for me.

I slipped the condom on over myself with one hand, and poured a generous amount of lube over it. I spread the lube onto my other hand and entered him with two fingers. He was one of the only boys I had ever been with who didn't seem to have a problem accommodating my size, but I wanted him warmed up and ready for me. A gentle fingering did the trick as his silky wet hole opened up to me nicely.

"Fuck me, Steel," he moaned, and my cock twitched in response.

We were both ready. I thrust into him with one direct, steady heave. He rocked his head back and bellowed. The fire that tore through him enflamed me too as we found our rhythm, our perfect pace.

Being inside him felt like arriving home after a long, cold, rainy day. I could finally relax because I knew I was exactly where I was meant to be. His tight hole took my every thrust, my every stretch, and enveloped my cock with a warmth that felt like the most natural and beautiful thing in the world.

I watched his head bucking wildly against the mattress. His eyes were closed and his mouth was letting loose a symphony of sounds of pure abandon. The noises he was making thrilled me. The sight of him turned me on more than I'd thought possible.

Suddenly, I had an idea. Something that would combine the feeling of closeness I had right now with the tenderness of the aftercare we had experienced earlier in the evening at Revolver.

I knew exactly what I wanted. I wanted Nick in my arms.

I slowly pulled out of him and his eyes opened, wide with surprise.

"What are you doing?" he asked.

I reached out and he placed his hands into mine.

"I want you in my arms," I said, as I walked over to the wall of my bedroom. "I want to fuck you standing up and hold you so close to me."

A look of worry crossed Nick's face.

"Uh, are you sure you can...you know, support all of...this?" he said, looking down at his body.

I lifted my biceps into the air and flexed them, showing them off with a proud grin.

"I think these bad boys will have you covered, baby." This time, I didn't care about the tongue slip, and judging by his smile, neither did he.

"In that case..." Nick began, and before he could finish the sentence he had hurled himself into the air...and into my arms.

I landed with a heavy thud against the wall, but having Nick in my arms meant I didn't feel a thing. I gripped his legs tightly, as my cock pressed against his thigh. I slowly twisted my body so that my cock found its way to his hole.

I pushed off the wall and turned us around, so that Nick was the one who had back support. He wrapped his feet tightly around my waist as I began to drill into him with my tongue and my cock. Holding him like this, suspended in mid-air, felt incredible.

I increased my pace, really feeling it in my legs as I plunged further and further into him.

My baby.

My...boy.

Our mouths opened and our tongues wrestled. His fingernails clawed into my shoulders. My cock was balls deep in him, thrusting into his tightness.

We were both getting close. I wanted us to come on the bed because I didn't want either one of us to move an inch after we did. I wanted our bodies wrapped up together for the rest of the night. Our bodies were calling out for it, they were craving it.

I pulled Nick away from the wall. All of his body weight was now bearing down on me. It was a little heavy, but hey, that's why I spent ten hours a week working out at the gym. It gave me the strength I needed to carry him to my bed.

Nick let out a surprised yelp, but after a few steps, he adjusted to it. In fact, he clamped down around my cock even harder, so that with every step I took, I plunged deeper and deeper into his tight hole.

"I like that," I whispered to him.

"It feels so fucking good," he replied straight away.

I was just a few feet away from the bed when my foot hitched on something. It must have been a shirt or some other item of clothing we'd torn off each other earlier and my foot gave way, my knee buckled as I lost my balance. Before I even knew what was happening, Nick flew out of my arms and hurtled at breakneck speed toward the floor. He landed on the carpet and let out an almighty roar.

I was down on the floor beside him nanoseconds later.

"Oh my god. Fuck, Nick. I'm so sorry. Are you okay?"

The agony twisted across his face as the pain spasmed throughout his body, thundering through and causing him to shake violently.

"It hurts, it hurts," he yelled out.

"Where? Show me."

"My ass." He grimaced with such discomfort I thought my heart would rip itself in two. What had I just done to him? "I broke my ass."

"Nick, try to stop moving," I said as I got up.

His eyes widened, glazed with a heavy cloud of bewilderment. One moment our bodies had been rocking and vibrating against each other, wrapped up in a cocoon of heavenly contentment, the next he had been hurled onto the floor...by me. Fuck!

"Where are you going?" The panic and fear was unmissable in his voice.

"To get my phone. I'm calling an ambulance. We need to get you to the ER."

"Nooooo," his scream sent a cold shiver through my sweat-drenched skin.

"Nick, we need to get help. Professional help. You're hurt."

I didn't add *because of me*. I bit down hard on my lower lip. How could I have done this? He was only just beginning to trust me and I'd fucked up in this most spectacular of ways.

"I'm okay," he said, clearly not okay. He tried to sit up a little and winced in pain at the slight movement.

"Nick, you are not okay," I said, lunging down onto the floor next to him. "We need to get help. I'll make the call, but can you please, please try and stay still?"

His big brown eyes welled with tears. "I don't want to go to the hospital. This is so...so embarrassing for me, Steel."

I bit down on my tongue as hard as I could. This wasn't his fault, it was mine. Purely mine. But at the same time, he was the one bearing the brunt of my fuck up. And he'd be the one being examined and stared at by everyone if we had to go outside. Which was why we wouldn't go.

"Nick, this is my fault. Not yours. I'm calling my doctor." I pressed my finger to his lips, cutting off his protest. "And the doctor will come here. To us. Okay? We are not leaving or going anywhere."

I felt his warm breath hit my face as he exhaled a sigh of relief.

"Okay," he agreed, and I ran to get my phone.

Doctor Polson was examining Nick what felt like a lifetime later, but really, the man had made it to my apartment in under fifteen minutes. He was a long-standing member at Revolver and, while not necessarily in my closest circle, he was someone I held in regard and knew we could trust.

"You will have to go and get an x-ray at some point," he said with a concerned look on his face as he shot me a glance. "I really can't rule anything in or out until then, but at this stage—and without an x-ray," he repeated with a strong emphasis, "it looks like a sprained tailbone. It could be a fracture but given that you're telling me the pain has subsided..." He looked at Nick who nodded his head at the doctor. "...it's most likely that."

Nick had been able to move into the bed and was lying there on his side, the pain relief meds from Dr. Polson having kicked in.

"What's the treatment for that?" I asked as he and I got up and moved to the door.

"We can treat the pain with the meds I gave you. The instructions are on the packet. Follow them. Other than that, just rest. It will heal in time. But, Steel," he said as he gently grabbed my forearm and tugged me away from the bed. "Make sure he gets an x-ray, please. We need to be able to rule out anything more serious."

"Oh, we will. I promise," I said, and the man's nerves seemed to lessen a little.

"Look, I think I have a sense of what happened here." I shot him a look and he clarified. "I mean, I don't know the specifics, of course. But judging by the fact that you called me, you don't want to go to the hospital, and he's naked, I assume it was something...sex related?"

I nodded my head and looked down. It sounded so clinical, and I felt like the biggest idiot in the world. It was all my fault.

"I know it seems embarrassing. But believe me, medical staff have seen everything. Take him to the Daylesford Medical Clinic. It's small. It's private and they're very understanding."

I nodded.

"Tomorrow," Dr. Polson added. I knew he was right, and tomorrow I would make sure we got medical treatment.

But right now, I had a hurt boy lying in my bed.

CHAPTER THIRTEEN

NICK

It's funny how quickly life can change.

One minute you think the most embarrassing moment of your life was the time you peed your pants in third grade, and the next, you're lying naked in someone's bed after a doctor has examined you because you got dropped on the floor while having sex.

Madonna was right in the '80s...life is a mystery.

Steel was walking the doctor out, which gave me a moment to try and compose myself. The best news was that the pain was subsiding. I mean, it was still there, but my back didn't feel like it was on fire anymore. It was manageable, and as long as I stayed relatively still, I could keep it in check.

But as the physical pain went down, another kind of pain flared up. The emotional kind. As a plus-size person, getting dropped wasn't just embarrassing. It was next-level mortifying. Along with my fear of spiders and a world without Beyoncé, getting dropped was near the top of my *I don't ever want this to happen in my life* list. But here we were.

"Hey." Steel's voice filled the room, followed by footsteps coming closer to the bed. To me lying like a big old loser in the bed.

"How are you feeling? Can I get you anything?" Steel sat down gingerly on the edge of the bed, careful not to make it move in any way. His face was painted with pain, his light blue eyes were studying me as if he were trying to guess what I might be needing. I wished *I* knew what I needed.

"I think I'm okay for now," I replied, and forced a smile. "Would you mind covering me with a sheet, please?"

"Of course." Steel shot up and a moment later, covered me gently with the sheet. He raised the bed cover halfway up my body, too. "Would you like it all the way up?" he asked.

I shook my head carefully.

"No thanks," I replied. "That's perfect right there."

"Nick," Steel began as he let out a breath. "I cannot even begin to tell you how sorry I am. This is all my fault. I slipped on something on the floor. It had nothing to do with..."

Ah, that awkward pause whenever someone came close to that awkward f-word.

Fat.

"It's okay—" I started to speak, but was quickly interrupted.

"Please let me finish," Steel said.

His eyes stilled and he chewed on his lower lip before he spoke again. When he did, his voice carried genuine conviction.

"This is not because of your size, Nick. Okay? I need you to know that. *I* was holding you up against the wall just fine. *I* was walking and carrying you just fine. Until *I*, emphasis on *I*, slipped. What happened was entirely my fault." He looked at me and I could see the sorrow filling his eyes.

"I dropped you because I slipped and for that..."

I looked at the man and his eyes were glassy. Was he about to cry? He cleared his throat and managed to croak out the last two words.

"I'm sorry."

How the hell do you respond to that? I was floored...for the second time that night. This time, though, at least it was a slightly better feeling, and one that wouldn't require medical attention.

"Hey," I said, and he looked up immediately. "Thank you, Steel. You have no idea how much I needed to hear that."

He couldn't have. He couldn't have known how much those words did to wash away the shame and downright awfulness that I was feeling right now. And he was absolutely right. It was just an accident. It had nothing to do with my size.

I took a few deep calming breaths, and he did too. Okay, I'd had my meltdown, now it was time for my panic attack.

My ass was literally my livelihood. How could I be a naked butler if I couldn't walk? How could I continue my reign as one of Daylesfords best-est go-go dancers if I couldn't dance? And how the fuck could I continue my forays into erotic cake-sitting with a sprained tailbone?

All of my work required an ass, and my ass was broken—and about to be broke.

Oh shit, my grandparents' bakery. How was I going to continue supporting them if I couldn't make any money? The thought of them having to close their bakery down after forty-five years was not a defeat I was prepared to accept, even in my current state.

"What are you thinking?" Steel probed gently. "You look like something's on your mind."

"Do I?" I had a thinking face? Who knew.

"Yeah, you look worried...and panicked."

I guessed there was no point in hiding it from him. I mean, he knew about my work and was fine with it. I blew out a breath and proceeded to tell him my concerns. I started off generally, talking about needing to support myself. Pay rent, cover expenses, keep a healthy inventory of strawberry bubblegum, that sort of thing.

But the funny thing was, that didn't really bother me all that much. Sure, I had to figure it out and I would. I always did. I was a survivor and I always found a way to get by. Always had, and I knew I always would.

But when it came to my grandparents, the people who had given up their lives to raise me, that was something else. The thought of them losing everything, now *that* was soul-crushing. I had to be strong for them. They needed me, there was no one else in our small family to help.

"What is it?" Steel asked.

He had scooted over and was sitting cross-legged on the bed close to me. He reached out and began to rub my forearm, the gentle friction making me feel snuggled and warm.

"It's my grandparents," I said.

"Do you live with them?" he asked, his eyes narrowing, his chin lifting.

"No, not anymore. But they raised me. My dad left before I was born and my mom has *issues*, shall we say, so they stepped in and stepped up in a major way."

"Wow, that's amazing," Steel said. "I mean, I'm sorry to hear about your parents, that part is awful, but your grandparents sound like they're pretty great people."

"They are," I said, smiling wistfully. "The best. And now it's my turn to look after them, and I can't."

"What do you mean by look after them?" Steel asked.

"They own a bakery down in the East Village."

"Oh yeah, I know that part of town. It's meant to be the next big thing."

I scoffed. "Yeah? Maybe that's why they've got developers practically forcing them to sell up. It sucks, Steel. That bakery is their life. It's my life, too. And it means nothing to greedy people with dollar signs in their eyes, you know?"

"It does suck," Steel said as he continued brushing up and down my arm, his gaze fixated on the movement. "That's why I got out of corporate law. If you think those developers are greedy assholes, wait till you meet the lawyers who represent them."

"They're...worse?" I guessed.

He nodded and briefly looked up at me before drawing his eyes back to my forearm.

"Like, ten times worse. I knew that wasn't for me, but I love the law. And I love helping people, so it made sense to start my own firm."

Hmm...

My heart warmed hearing Steel talk. His voice had that tone again, that tone that meant he was telling the truth. I knew he was, I could feel it. I always trusted my gut when it came to people, and I was always right about stuff like this.

But then a little niggle rose in the back of my mind. He wasn't telling the whole truth though, was he? There was a little something he was conveniently leaving out. Something along the lines of, *I started my own law firm...with the money I had in my trust fund.* I mean, starting a law firm couldn't have been cheap. How else could he have done it?

I pushed aside all the warring thoughts battling inside my head and focused again on my immediate fuckery.

"I'm helping my grandparents, Steel," I said. "I'm working my ass off and putting all my spare money into that bakery. But now...my ass is literally broken."

"Sprained," he was quick to correct as he shot me a stiff look. "And I don't care what you say, Nick. I am putting my foot down and we are going to the hospital tomorrow to get it checked out. Properly."

Okay, Mr. Bossy Daddy.

I could deal with that. He was right, we did need to get it checked out. I wanted that, too. I just couldn't deal with the shock of what had happened and then being out in public so quickly afterwards. I was fine to go out in the morning.

"Yes, I agree. I would like to make sure that my ass is only sprained and not broken." I didn't mean it in a bitchy way, but I could see Steel wincing at my words.

"There is another thing I'm going to put my foot down about, Nick," he said as he stopped rubbing my arm and looked me straight in the eyes. "And I have a feeling you might not like it."

"And what might that be?" I said with an arched eyebrow.

"Until you're better, you're staying here with me. This is my fault. I am taking responsibility for what happened and I am going to look after you until you get better."

"What if I don't want to stay here?" I asked defensively. I tried to sit up a little, but a jolt of pain stabbed at my back and stopped me in my tracks.

"I don't care," Steel said, keeping his eyes on me. "I can see that you're in pain just trying to sit up. I am not going to burden you, or Mikey, or your grandparents with having to look after you. I want to do it."

Silence. A stare-off. A major stare-off. Brown eyes versus light blue.

Some staggered breathing. That was me. I think the meds were starting to wear off. I was trying to remember the lyrics to Destiny's Child *Survivor* to throw in Steel's face, but my memory was a little foggy.

Okay, the meds were deffers wearing off. I would just have to tell Steel he could shove it up his ass in a less musical way, and that was what I was about to do when he spoke again.

No roughness.

No assholeness.

No *I'm better than you and I'm throwing money at the problem to fix it*-ness.

Just...a kind and genuine plea.

"Please let me do this, Nick. It's important to me."

I narrowed my eyes. There was a steely determination behind those baby blues.

"If you say no," he continued, "I will respect it. I won't like it and

I'm warning you now, I will call and text you non-stop, but I will accept it."

He was playing with the sheet and not looking at me.

"But I would really, *really* like for you to please consider my offer," he said, and looked up.

The hopefulness in his eyes filled my chest with a feeling of...something. I wasn't sure what, exactly. Everything about him was confusing me.

As much as I hated to admit it, the man had a point. Several of them. I mean, even if I were able to walk myself out of here, where would I go? The truth was, I would need some help, at least for a little while.

Two of the things that I hated the most in the world were being a burden and asking for help. I couldn't ask my grandparents to look after me, they had done more than enough. Besides, they were already plenty busy just trying to keep the bakery afloat.

I couldn't ask Mikey for help, either. I mean, I could have, and I'm sure he would have taken me in, but I just really didn't like doing that. I ran through a list of names of my other friends in my head and dismissed each one for the very same reason.

And yet, here I was with someone offering to help me. I didn't even have to ask—the offer had come from him. It was genuine and it did kinda make sense. He was there when it happened and now he wanted to be there to help me get better.

But I was still so confused about everything. The part of me that hated needing help was in a screaming match with the part of me that just wanted to accept Steel's offer. What was I supposed to do?

Steel's eyes hadn't left my face for who knew how long, and it felt...good. Maybe I could give this a try? It might be nice to be the one who got looked after, rather than the one who looked after everyone else. Maybe just once...?

"Okay," I finally said, trying to hold down all of the emotions that were bubbling inside of me. "I'll stay here until I get better. I will let you look after me, Steel."

Relief washed over Steel's face as he broke into a wide smile.

"Thank you, Nick," he said, letting out a deep breath. "I will take care of you like you have never been taken care of before. I promise. Whatever you want, whatever you need..."

"'Cause I'm every woman..." I belted out in my best Whitney Houston impression. My rendition was met with a surprised look and a furrowed brow. "Wait, you weren't just quoting Whitney Houston's *I'm Every Woman*?"

"Uh, no...I wasn't," he said as a dry smile returned to his lips. "But I like that that's where you went with that. I love how your mind works, Nick."

"What can I say?" I said with a gentle, single-shoulder shrug. "I'm a diva. And you can never, ever hold a good diva down."

CHAPTER FOURTEEN

STEEL

There's a well-known saying that when people tell you who they are, you should believe them. When Nick Macklin said he was a diva, I should have believed him.

How one person could take up all of the space in a six-thousand-square-foot penthouse, I will never know. But over the course of the past two weeks, that's exactly what he'd done. Nick had single handedly turned my life upside down.

From his requests for yolk-less omelettes (after I had made them with yolks), to his commentary on the type of laundry softener I was using (apparently I was a monster because it had too much lavender, so yes, I threw it out and bought an unscented brand), to the way he would wave his arms around in the air while listening to music on his phone (he didn't want to get behind on his dancing practice), Nick was clearly making the most of my offer to look after him.

He was one of a kind.

He was maddening.

He was irrational and stubborn.

He was more than just a boy, he was a brat.

He was the brat I wanted to spend the rest of my life with.

I knew it from the moment he threw himself into my arms the night of the accident, and as weird as it sounds, I knew it even more the moment he fell out of them. Nick brought out something in me that made me feel things I hadn't known were possible to feel.

I had been with boys before. Quite a few of them, actually. I was no Porter, but I was also no prude. I had felt *attraction* to guys in the past, even liked a guy or two, but I'd never felt anything like *this*.

It was a need more than just a feeling. In the same way that I needed air to breathe, I needed Nick in my life.

Just by being here in my house, he made me realize how unfulfilling my life had become. Sure, I had the firm, and I was genuinely proud of the good work we were doing. And yes, I had friends, and I had the community at Revolver. But I didn't have *him*.

But let me back it up a little.

First things first, the very next day I marched Nick—as gently as I could, because he was still in a bit of pain—to the emergency room at the Daylesford Medical Clinic. After a full round of x-rays and scans, I was elated when we were told it was just a sprain, like Dr. Polson had suspected. And thankfully, a mild sprain at that. It would heal on its own, which we were told should happen within two to four weeks.

Which was just the right amount of time I needed to make Nick fall madly in love with me. First, I'd help him heal his sprained ass, then I'd find a way to mend his broken heart.

For someone so loud and who only ever kept his mouth shut when he was sleeping, Nick had said surprisingly little about his love life. But from the titbits he had offered, I got the sense that men found Nick to be a lot to handle.

He *was* a lot to handle.

And I loved it. After we returned from the hospital and realized that we had gotten off relatively scot-free, the playful-slash-bratty side of Nick returned with a vengeance.

It wasn't anything big, it was just the million-and-one little things that he did from the moment he woke up until his head hit the pillow at night, that continued the gymnastics happening inside of my chest.

Part of it was real. There was a real sassiness to him that was just who he was. But part of it was a cover, a mask for the things he didn't want to show the world. For the things that he didn't want to show me.

He had opened up a little by telling me about his grandparents raising him and the way he was supporting them in running their bakery. I loved the way his eyes twinkled when he talked about them. There was real love there. And I loved finding out that the reason he was working so hard was to help them. That was another thing we had in common: a good work ethic.

But after he had done that, I noticed him clamming up again. It was like he had said too much, so he quickly retreated into the comfort of hiding behind his cocky, confident demeanor.

I was determined to find out more about him. I wanted to know everything. To do that, I knew I had to earn his trust.

He had been truly wonderful about the accident. I still couldn't think about it without feeling a surge of anger rising through me at how stupid and careless I had been. Thank God he wasn't seriously injured. I don't know how I would have lived with myself if something really bad had happened to him.

Instead, I fussed and fretted over him 'like his grandma did', as he took great pleasure in pointing out to me—on numerous occasions each day. I didn't care. I had made a promise that I would look after him like he had never been looked after before.

I was a man of my word.

I didn't lie, I didn't put up with bullshit, and when I said I was going to do something, you could bet your bottom dollar that I would do it.

And you know what? Looking after him felt so good. In a way, I realized that it was a type of aftercare. Obviously without the sex component preceding it, because that was unfortunately off the table until he fully recovered. But it had all the aftercare elements I loved so much: taking time, giving attention, and really communicating.

The funny thing was, I didn't think Nick realized just how much he liked it, too. I mean, I was the one who told him what aftercare was, but the way he smiled, or preened, or leaned into me whenever I was looking after him, confirmed that on a deeper level, we were both on the same page.

Now all I had to do was find a way to make him see that too.

"Steel!" Nick's voice roared through the apartment, accompanied by the tinkling of the brass bell I had given him, jolting me back into reality. "Steel! I need youuuu."

I smiled as I walked from my home office into the living room where Nick was currently living what looked like his best life. There were trashy magazines, half-opened boxes of chocolates and chips, a DIY facial kit, bubble gum wrappers, and all sorts of other colourful bits and bobs strewn all over the place. Whatever kept Nick occupied and happy while he was recovering on the sofa was fine with me.

"Yes, baby?" I said as I walked over to him.

His brows pinched together tightly. It always intrigued me, how his face responded differently each time I called him *baby*. Were his emotions so much of a rollercoaster that they changed everyday, sometimes a number of times during the day? Or did he really not know what he was thinking or feeling about me yet?

I wasn't sure, but either way, I knew I had his consent. When the word *baby* slipped out again for the fourth or fifth time on the first day he was with me, I asked him about it point blank. Did he mind me calling him baby? His response? A shrug, a finger wag, and four softly spoken words.

"No, I like it."

I let him know that if at any time he did start to mind, he needed to tell me and I would stop straight away.

That moment hadn't come yet.

Nick's eyes were glued to his phone.

"It's saying it's here," he said, not looking up.

"Are you expecting something?" I asked.

He nodded. "Could you check for me, please?"

He lifted his head and batted those dark lashes of his. How the fuck could anyone resist that?

"Of course, baby," I said. "I'll call Tanner downstairs and ask him to check for deliveries."

"Thanks Da...dude."

Da-dude.

I cut off the chuckle in my throat. He'd done that a few times. Almost said Daddy, but caught himself at the last minute. Which was fair enough, we hadn't really had *that talk* yet. In fact, there were a few things we needed to discuss.

Was this just a convalescence thing? Me just helping him get back on his feet—literally—after the accident? What would happen once he was better? Would he just leave? A heavy pang hit my chest at the thought of it. I really didn't want that to happen.

Or were we moving into something else? Boyfriends? Friends? Daddy/boy territory? It was hard to tell. All I knew was that I wanted to get out of this *Da-dude* muddle as quickly as possible and try to get a better picture of where we were, and where we might be heading.

Because of his current condition, our physical affection was restricted to the occasional kiss and gentle stroking, usually arms or whatever part of his body was outside of the blanket he was under. Not the other kind of stroking, I'm afraid.

Tanner arrived a few moments later with a brown parcel addressed to Nick. I glanced down at it briefly and it warmed my chest to see his name at my address. It just looked right. I handed him the parcel and his eyes lit up like a star-filled sky.

"Ooh goody," he exclaimed. I loved seeing him like this. "Would you do this with me?"

His arms were a flurry of activity, hastily unwrapping whatever was inside the box.

"Uh, sure," I said, without any idea what I was agreeing to. If it meant spending time with Nick, I was in. It couldn't be anything too terrible, or so I thought until I saw a box plastered with a smiling Britney Spears looking back at me. "What is that?"

I cast a worried look Nick's way.

"It's a puzzle." Nick said it as if it were the most obvious thing in the world. "It's a Britney Spears puzzle. This is her 2000 – 2001 era. It's my favorite."

I nodded calmly, but inside, I had no idea what the heck he was talking about.

"And you, Steel Crawford," he said, resting the puzzle on his lap and flashing me his most mischievous grin. "You just agreed to do it with me."

"I, uh, wha—"

I saw him try to move himself toward the coffee table.

"Wait there," I said as I ran to his side. "Let me help you with that."

I was met with an eye roll. I'd gotten used to that.

"I can move my big ass from the sofa to the coffee table, you know?"

"Are you arguing with me, boy?" I friendly-growled at him.

Our faces were inches apart and I could see it as if it was happening in slow motion—how his beautiful, thick lips turned, tightened, and formed the sweetest pout I had ever seen.

"No," he said, leaning into me and letting me guide him toward the coffee table.

A few moments later, I had positioned him carefully and he was seated comfortably on the floor. There were a thousand pieces of Britney Spears on the table and I was lightly running my fingers over them, but unable to keep my eyes off Nick.

"Are you sure you want to do this with me?" I asked. "I don't really know much about Britney."

He giggled and it made his whole body shake a little. His hair was getting longer now, falling down past his shoulders. I loved seeing how it moved every time he turned his head.

"I'm pretty sure you don't need to know her entire back catalogue to be able to put together a puzzle, Steel."

Steel. The way he said my name sent a tingly warm sensation from my belly up to my torso. It made me feel a little giddy.

I chuckled and frowned at the same time. Nick noticed. Like he always did.

"I just like doing things with you, that's all," he said, trying to make it sound casual as his eyes flitted across all the puzzle pieces laid out before us. There was nothing casual about the way his words made my heart do cartwheels of joy.

"Oh yeah," I said, trying out this whole casual thing for myself. "And why's that?"

He smirked and looked up for the briefest of moments. He knew I was fishing. Would he bite?

He licked his lips. It wasn't suggestive, trust me, I knew *that* look. No, he was deep in thought, as if he were deciding whether to tell me something or not.

"You know what my favorite part about staying here is?" he finally asked.

"My wizardry in the kitchen and awesome omelette-making skills?" I said with a laugh.

"No," he smiled back. "It's this. Just hanging out with you like this. You and me...and a thousand pieces of Britney. Ooh, that rhymes!"

His whole face lit up at that and I threw my head back in laughter.

There was no denying it. Nick Macklin was the most unique boy in the world.

CHAPTER FIFTEEN

NICK

"I'm looking for a belly button ring. Steel, can you help me find it *please?*"

I looked over at Steel, sitting cross-legged on the floor, his tongue sticking out of the corner of his mouth, his eyes scouring the coffee table looking for anything but the one thing I needed.

"Uh, hello, earth to Steel," I said loudly enough to startle him. At least I got his attention.

"Sorry, sorry," he said, looking up and shooting me an adorable smile. "I was looking for the tip of her nose."

Was it wrong that seeing him so intently focused on doing something that he didn't want to do, but was doing for me, made me feel so good inside? Like, smelling a freshly baked apple pie kinda good?

Actually, I had been feeling pretty damn good for the two weeks I had been staying with him—sprained tailbone aside, that is. But that was healing nicely. I wasn't in pain anymore, thank god, because my pain threshold was pretty much capped at a paper cut. I would feel a little niggle once in a while if I got up or moved too quickly, but that was about it.

I leaned back and watched Steel for a moment. It was one of my favorite things to do, just looking at him when he didn't know I was doing it. I loved seeing him relaxed and unguarded like this. He was wearing his usual around-the-house outfit, his favorite faded jeans and a white shirt. What I loved even more was the fact that I knew he had an around-the-house outfit.

I also loved that he was at the house as much as he was. After we had gotten back from the hospital the day after the accident, he'd arranged to turn one of his spare rooms into a home office. His staff brought in everything he needed that day, which meant that he could work from home and look after me as he had promised to.

And boy, did the man look after me or what? This might come as a surprise, but I could be a little...high maintenance. Totally worth it, but high maintenance nonetheless. Not that Steel minded, or at least he didn't seem like he minded.

He cooked for me. He changed his laundry detergent for me. He even gave me a brass bell to ring whenever I needed him. And when I rang it, he would come and get me whatever I needed. That was really...special. It was something I could deffers get used to. I didn't care about him being rich and powerful, I cared that he dropped everything at the ring of a bell. For me.

And every time he did any one of those little things for me, my heart melted just a little bit more. I couldn't help it. He was just so sweet and thoughtful and caring and adorable. I loved his around-the-house outfit and the way he did things I knew he didn't want to do, like a thousand-piece Britney Spears puzzle.

I thought that when he offered for me to stay here, he would continue working in the office and maybe call me once or twice a day to make sure I was alright. Or maybe he'd occasionally send his assistant around to make sure I hadn't fallen into the toilet. That actually would have been fine.

I didn't expect him to uproot his life just for me. But he did anyway. Without me asking for any of it. The best part was that he never looked like having me here, taking over his place, his sofa, his bedroom, his bed, bothered or inconvenienced him for even the slightest moment.

"So," I said as I picked up something that kind of looked like a belly ring, squinting at the blurry blue-gray-ish piece, "tell me more about this case that you're working on for the developer."

"How did you know that?" he asked with a curious head tilt.

"I overheard you on the phone as I was walking to the bathroom. I wasn't eavesdropping," I clarified. "I mean, yes, I was checking you out because you do look pretty sexy in that office, but eavesdropping? No, not really my style."

A low laugh escaped his throat as his light blue eyes glanced up at me and I felt my heart flutter.

"They're a great company. Unlike the experience your grandparents are having with their developers, who sound like assholes, these guys are amazing."

"Well, it doesn't help my grandparents, but it's nice to know that there are at least some good developers out there."

"Oh, for sure there are," he said with a nod. "These guys are doing an amazing revitalization in the East Village, and they're doing it thoughtfully."

"What does that mean? Sorry, I'm not an expert architecturalist, or anything."

A funny look crossed Steel's face, like he was trying to suppress a smile or something, but I couldn't figure out why.

"I'm not an *architecturalist* either..." He kept grinning at me. Maybe I had something on my face? "...but it means that they're going to include things like plenty of green space, designated low-income housing, environmentally friendly designs, and even office space for nonprofits, including an LGBTQ center."

"Holy shit, that is amazing," I said. "Almost as amazing as you helping me find that goddamn belly button ring." I threw away the incorrect piece I had in my fingers and scowled as I glanced at the coffee table. I swear those thousand puzzle pieces had doubled when we weren't watching.

"I'm looking, I promise," Steel said, rummaging his slender fingers over the pieces.

"Oh hey," I said casually. "My grandma texted this morning. She's invited us for dinner in the next week or two. My grandparents want to meet the man who's looking after me."

"Oh," Steel looked up. "How do you feel about that?"

"I'm fine with it if you are," I said.

"Sounds good to me," he said with a smile. "I look forward to meeting them."

And just like that, it was done.

It wasn't a massively big deal, but then again, it kinda was.

Steel knew I didn't have my parents in my life, so meeting my grandparents was the next best thing, and yet, it didn't seem to bother him in the slightest. In fact, it seemed like he was actually looking forward to it. I chewed on my lower lip. I had no idea what to make of all of this.

"Look, I can't find your belly button ring, but can I get you a drink?" he asked, standing up. I nodded. "What would you like, baby?"

"Just a soda with a straw, please, Da...dude...Steel."

Fuck.

Another funny look, but again, he didn't say anything as he padded over to the kitchen.

Hmm, interesting how half a word can perfectly capture how completely confused I felt about Steel and the whole *thing* that was happening between us. He had totally caught me off guard when he asked if he could call me 'baby'. Funny, because I didn't second guess myself then. I said yes straight away because it just felt right.

And I'd been feeling all sorts of right over the last two weeks of living with him. More than right, actually. I felt at ease. He made me happy.

So why the fuck couldn't I call him 'Daddy'? I knew that was what he wanted. I could tell. And it was what I wanted, too, but I was scared.

I wasn't your typical boy.

I didn't behave.

I wasn't compliant.

And I wasn't a size zero. In other words, I was no Mikey.

Don't get me wrong, I loved my best friend more than anything in the world, and I loved the dynamic he had with Stirling. But Mikey was a good boy. Sure, he had his own opinions and made his own decisions, but he let his Daddy take control, as well. He needed that as much as Stirling needed it, and honestly, it was the most beautiful thing in the world to see.

It's just, that kind of dynamic wouldn't work for me. I wasn't that boy and I didn't want that Daddy. I was loud. I was big. I was unfiltered, and I was *a lot*. No Daddy had ever been able to handle me. Not all of me.

As much as I liked Steel—more and more with each day that I spent with him—I didn't want him to become another one of those Daddies that thought they could handle me before they realized it was all just too much.

That *I* was too much.

I stared absently out the massive windows. The city was cloudy and gray.

"So, you think I'm pretty sexy when I'm sitting in my office, huh?" Steel said, returning with my soda and straw.

Ooh, pink, my favorite! He remembered.

"Thank you," I said, taking the drink from him. "Yeah, I do. I think you're pretty sexy in your office. In the kitchen. Sitting here on the floor. Standing behind me while you're fucking the living daylights out of me."

If looking at Steel when he didn't know I was looking at him was my favorite thing to do, seeing the man's facial expressions when I came out with some of my crazier shit was a close second.

He did this thing where his mouth would gape open and his chin would drop to his chest slowly, almost exaggeratedly. It looked like his head was about to fall off his neck and it was the cutest thing ever.

"Uh, we, uh, I mean..."

I burst out laughing. He was too cute.

"What? I'm horny," I said. "And I am feeling better, so, you know..." Steel's eyebrows shot up excitedly.

I let the words float in the air between us.

"What are you saying, Nick?" Steel asked, taking a gulp of his water.

"I need a cock inside of me."

More water gulping.

"Uh huh..."

"I need your cock inside me, Steel. Now!"

If Steel's coffee table didn't weigh like two tons, I was sure he would have flipped it over and lunged at me. Instead, being the considerate gentleman that he was, he walked over to me, arms outstretched, and helped me up onto the sofa. Carefully and gently.

But I didn't want careful and gentle, and I certainly didn't want a gentleman.

It had been two weeks. I wanted a hard, rough, *pull my hair and slap my ass* kinda fucking.

"We have to take it slow," Steel said.

"I don't want slow," I replied.

"You have to listen to me...boy."

"Okay..."

"No fucking today. You're not ready yet."

"I am," I protested. If I were standing, I would have been stomping my feet right about now.

"Your body is not ready yet, baby," Steel said as he traced his fingers along the side of my face.

"But I need it. I need *you*." I didn't care if I sounded whiny or desperate. Truth was, I really did need him inside of me. More than he knew, more than I could tell him.

"Sounds like," Steel said as he shuffled down off the sofa and sank onto the floor, "my baby needs release."

He unzipped my pants and gently pulled them down my meaty thighs.

"Oh yeah," I breathed, lying back and letting my body press into the plushness of the sofa. I didn't need to be an Einstein to figure out where this was heading.

He cupped my balls in his warm hands as he took my cock in his mouth. I let out a deep moan. It was a pent-up, *I haven't come once in two weeks* kinda moan. My balls were heavy, aching, and so, so full.

His warm, wet mouth felt amazing sliding up and down my cock. He flicked his tongue under the head and a fierce shiver tore through my spine. I writhed my back in pleasure and suddenly, it hurt. It wasn't a lot. It wasn't a sharp or stabbing pain. But it was there.

I propped myself up onto my elbows and pressed my back into the couch to stabilize myself. That did the trick.

"What's wrong?" Steel's light blue eyes were focused on me like lasers. "Something's wrong, I can feel it."

"It's nothing, I just felt a little bit of pain in my back, so I've moved. And I'm fine now," I added quickly.

Steel's face crumpled in concern, but there was no way in hell I wanted this to stop.

"Are you sure you're okay? We can stop right now."

"If you stop right now," I said in my most serious voice, "I will literally die."

Steel chuckled again. "Well, we can't have that now, can we? But no more big crazy movements, okay?"

I nodded. "Okay. Now shut up and suck my cock."

Steel's mouth gaped open in shock. I used that as an opportunity to thrust my dick a little closer to his face. Not a subtle hint, but one that he understood straight away, and got him working away, bobbing up and down on my cock just like before.

It didn't take long for my balls to tighten and that familiar feeling of release to push through me.

"I'm close," I said, meeting Steel's gaze.

The man looked so good with my cock stuffed in his mouth, but he looked even better gazing up at me with my cock stuffed in his mouth.

He kept going, wrapping his fingers around the base of my cock and swallowing harder, encouraging me to come.

When I did, when I felt the release pummel me from the inside out, I didn't scream. I didn't shout. I didn't twist and flail my arms around. I was shaking a little, but I was silent.

So was Steel.

Our eyes were locked. Blue eyes on brown. Silent. Still. Super-fucking-sexy.

After a few moments, Steel slowly slid my cock out of his mouth, tilting his head back to swallow the last of my release.

"That was a lot," he said, holding back a cough as he made his way over to me.

"Sorry, I haven't come in two weeks. I guess it would be a lot."

He snuggled in next to me, the heat from his body warming me up too.

"It was a lot," Steel agreed, snuggling even closer.

"I'm a lot," I said.

"You are a lot," Steel said, nuzzling his nose into my neck. "But I like that. And I like you...a lot."

CHAPTER SIXTEEN

STEEL

"You know, you didn't have to wear a tie," Nick said as he turned to face me on his grandparents' porch.

"I'm meeting your grandparents," I said, fidgeting with it to get it just right. "Of course I do. Besides, you think I look fucking hot in a suit and tie."

"Oh, do I now?" Wide brown eyes. Hands on hips. Cocky head snap.

Yeah, Nick was back to his good ol' self again. It had been a full month since the accident, and yesterday's x-ray had given us the news we were both hoping for. His sprain had healed up beautifully and there was no permanent damage done.

"Yes, you do," I said, patting down the front of my shirt and squaring my shoulders. "But let's save the dirty talk for later."

"You started it." Nick shot me a cheeky grin. "Besides, since I got the all-clear, I want to do more than just talk dirty with you later."

Desire filled my body at Nick's words, but I just smiled and looked at him. I couldn't wait to be inside of him again. But his grandparents' porch was not the place for this conversation, or for the barrage of filthy thoughts running through my head.

Greenhill was your typical suburban neighborhood filled with rows and rows of slightly older houses on decent-sized blocks.

"You ready?" he asked as he lifted his hand to knock on the front door.

I nodded. I was. I knew this was a big deal for him. Not that he had said it was, because of course he wouldn't. But I could tell. I got the feeling he hadn't invited many guys to meet his grandparents.

I may have been feeling a little nervous myself, and I wanted to make a good impression, hence the suit and tie, but Nick was just as jittery and just as keen to make sure this evening went well. I could see it in the way he'd changed outfits a million times, finally settling on a smart maroon and black plaid shirt and dark jeans that clung to his ass in all sorts of wicked ways.

And in the way he'd checked his phone a million times to make sure we weren't running late on the drive over.

And in the way he'd smiled and his eyes had softened when he saw me grab the wine I had bought for his grandparents as a *hello and please don't hate me for breaking your grandson's ass* gift.

Nick gave a quick knock and a few moments later, a gray-haired man with a friendly face opened the door and pulled him in for a hug.

"Gramps," Nick said, giving the man a bear hug.

When they pulled apart, the man gave me a not-so-discreet look up and down. He was well dressed himself, in navy blue pants and a checkered red and black shirt with a high collar. I was glad I hadn't given in to Nick's ribbing and had stuck with wearing a suit and tie. First impressions mattered.

"Mr. Macklin, it's great to meet you. I've heard so many good things about you," I said, pressing my palm firmly into his, holding his gaze the whole time. He had Nick's brown eyes—or rather, Nick had his.

"Call me Ray, please," he said as he invited me in with a warm smile.

"Grandma," Nick's voice rang out happily at the sight of his grandma walking out of the kitchen to greet us. I could see her smile over Nick's shoulder as they hugged. Her light brown hair was pulled back in a bun and her face looked soft and gentle.

They both seemed so typical, living in a typical house in a typical suburb. I didn't know what I had been expecting, all I knew was that Nick was anything but typical. I thought there'd be at least a little bit of eccentricity, something different and *out there* about them. Maybe they were former hippies who had lived in a commune, or reformed motorcycle-club members who had settled down to start a family.

But no. They seemed to be your everyday grandma and grandpa. The picture of normal wholesomeness.

Nick's grandma—Millie, as she insisted I call her—was thrilled with the red wine I gave her. "It'll go perfectly with the lamb I'm making," she said appreciatively, flashing me a genuine smile. "I hope you're both hungry."

I studied the house as we were led into the dining room, which was next to the kitchen. It was a decent size and had a warm, lived-in feel to it. I was searching for signs of Nick—his messiness, his colorfulness—but there was nothing out of the ordinary in the entrance, or the living room we walked past on the way to the dining room. Until we sat down and I spied a few silver frames on a bookshelf in the corner of the room.

"Are there any embarrassing photos of Nick you'd like me to see?" I said, looking at Ray.

Nick let out an exaggerated *"oh my god"* and a dramatic eye roll, but his grandfather simply smiled playfully back at me. I knew that cheeky grin, too. Between his big brown eyes, his bushy brows, and the smile that lit up his whole face, he was basically Nick in forty years' time. That thought settled happily in my stomach.

Nick's grandparents were absolutely lovely and the conversation, as well as the wine, flowed freely for the rest of the evening.

Until dessert. That was when things came to a screeching halt.

Not that anyone noticed. None of them could have possibly known. But it made me sweat like a turkey at Thanksgiving, and I had a sinking feeling that it would ruin everything that was happening between Nick and me.

It was just one innocent suggestion that triggered the tsunami of despair in me.

Nick's grandmother had made the most delicious lemon shortbread cookies I had ever tasted.

"The secret ingredient is coconut flakes," she told me when I commented on how good they were. "And," she said, lifting a white saucer she had placed in the middle of the table, "homemade chocolate dipping sauce. Just drizzle it over the cookies and you'll be in heaven."

That. That was it. Blink and you'd miss it, right?

That innocent little dessert-eating suggestion was the thing that changed everything.

It made Ray drop his spoon angrily into his bowl.

It turned Millie's face sour with regret, like she'd just swallowed a lemon.

And it made my heart stop dead in its tracks.

"What's the matter with you two?" Nick asked his grandparents. "Why are you looking so weird all of a sudden?"

"I'm sorry," Ray said, looking at me as a gentle flush filled his cheeks. "I don't mean to be rude, but that word...we don't like that word being used around here, do we, Millie?"

Nick's grandma shook her head and looked down into her lap, seeming sorry she had ever uttered it.

"What word?"

I was glad Nick asked. I wanted to know myself, but I wasn't sure if it would have been appropriate for me to probe.

"Drizzle." They both said it at the same time.

"Drizzle?" Nick and I queried in unison.

"It's a long story," Millie said as she scooped a mouthful of cookie—sans chocolate sauce—into her mouth and carefully chewed it.

"I don't know if Nick has told you, but we're having trouble with some developers looking to take our bakery out from under us," Ray said, and I could see the anger brewing in his eyes.

I put my spoon down and folded my hands on the table.

"He has," I said. "And I'm really sorry you're going through that. If there's anything my firm can do to help, please let me know."

"You've already done so much," Millie said as Ray nodded his head firmly in agreement.

Nick glanced at me with a quirked eyebrow, but I quickly looked away from him and turned my attention back to his grandparents.

"Wait," Nick said. "What does the word *drizzle* have to do with the asshole developers? I'm totally confused."

That made both of us.

"Language, Nick," Ray scolded him, half playfully, half seriously.

"The name of the developers is Drizzle & Co," Millie explained.

"What a fu...what a stupid name," Nick deftly corrected himself as he took another mouthful.

I suddenly lost my appetite as my body slammed into a giant granite wall of panic.

Drizzle & Co were the developers my firm was representing.

I'd had no idea they were the same developers that Nick's grandparents were having issues with until right that very moment. Nick had never mentioned their name, he had clearly only just heard it for the first time, too.

From the way he had talked about them, I never in a million

years would have thought we were talking about the same company. Drizzle & Co couldn't be the greedy asshole developers that Nick's grandparents were dealing with. It didn't make any sense...

"You alright, Steel?" Millie asked, looking at me.

"Uh, yeah, I'm fine," I said, swallowing down around the choking sensation clogging my throat. I had to quiet the frenzied stampede of panicked thoughts racing through my mind and somehow, *somehow* get through the rest of the evening.

Maybe there was some way of explaining it to Nick so that he would understand? Oh man, who was I kidding? Nick adored his grandparents more than anything else, there was no way in the world he would understand any of this. I was doomed.

When his grandparents refused our offer to clear the table, doing it themselves instead, it was the first time Nick and I had been alone all evening.

As soon as they were out of sight, he squeezed my thigh and leaned over to whisper, "Don't get tired on me, Steel." A mischievous grin stretched across his lips. "Because you have a month's worth of fucking to make up for when we get back."

The evening wrapped up shortly after that. Nick's grandparents were early risers, getting up at four each morning to open their bakery. And Nick? Well, he had other things on his mind, and I didn't think he cared what time we got up tomorrow, judging by the hungerlust flashing in his eyes every time he looked my way.

We had barely walked through my front door when Nick wrapped his hands around my neck and pulled me in for a hard, sloppy, furious kiss.

My mind was torn. Should I tell Nick and risk losing him, or carry the heavy burden of keeping this secret from him? But with each passing second that his tongue was lashing around wildly in my mouth, my body was succumbing to my desire for him.

I didn't want this to stop.

I didn't want this to be the last time we had sex, either. But I knew full well that it could be. So, I was going to make love to him—to this completely unique, captivating, and devilishly beautiful boy—as if I would never get the chance again.

We tumbled into bed.

I was determined to resist Nick's pressure to hurry up. No, I wanted to savor this. I wanted to relish and remember every touch, every moan, every sweet taste of his body on my lips forever.

"What are you doing, Steel? Hurry up and fuck me," Nick breathed urgently into my ear.

Okay, it wasn't exactly Shakespeare, but it still warmed my heart more than I could describe.

I took my time. I slipped both of us out of our clothes and kissed Nick long and hard. Our naked bodies lay next to each other in my big bed, joined by the glistening heads of our cocks rubbing against each other.

I was gentle. Nick had gotten the all-clear, but we weren't about to jump into any sort of advanced tantric positions anytime soon. I kissed and nibbled and caressed and stroked every inch of his beautiful, firm, soft body.

And when I was finally inside him, I was quiet. Apart from the occasional soft moans coming out of his mouth and the sound of my balls slapping against his ass, there was no other sound in the room. The silence was our sanctuary as I stared into his eyes, my hips thrusting harder against his body.

His body relaxed as he took all of me, with both of us on our sides. His warmth pulled me further inside. He was intoxicating. His open mouth, his gently rocking head, his thick hair that I was dragging my fingers through and that left the sweet scent of him lingering on my fingertips.

We both came at the same time and it was a blissful surrender.

I pulled his back to my chest and held him tight, not wanting to let him go. Not wanting my cock to leave his body.

When I finally pulled out of him, a cold shiver ran through me. I helped him up to the top of the bed and placed a blanket over him. His face looked peaceful, glimmering in a haze of thin sweat and a whole bunch of post-sex-high endorphins that were rushing through his body. They were rushing through my body, too.

"Worth the wait?" I asked, cradling my arms around his body to spoon him.

"Oh yeah," he sighed over his shoulder. "But let's never wait a month again, okay?"

I frowned and the heavy wall of panic returned, settling in my gut. He was talking about a future that might never happen.

"Nick, I don't want you to move out." My voice was barely more than a whisper, but his ear was right next to my mouth so I knew he'd hear me. "I want you to stay here with me. Please stay here with me. Don't leave me."

He shuffled his body, pressing harder into mine. The heat coming off him was warmer than the blanket covering us both.

"Okay," he said. "I'll stay with you, Steel."

Relief flooded through me. Even if it was temporary, even if it would all be taken away from me tomorrow, right now, at this very moment, he was here with me—and he was mine.

A single tear made its way down my cheek and dropped into his messy brown hair. He didn't feel it. I couldn't tell if he was awake or drifting into sleep.

"I love you, Nick Macklin."

CHAPTER SEVENTEEN

NICK

"Uh...a little help, please?" Mikey said, his voice coming from somewhere around the mountain-high pile of brown boxes lined up by Steel's front door.

"I am helping," I said, waving my hand in the air to silence him as I furiously texted Steel back. Because, you see, over the course of the last week, I had discovered something.

I was an addict.

It was a new addiction, but it had taken hold of me real bad. It was one that I couldn't stop. One that I had no intention of stopping. It was so strong that it had me in its powerful grip after just the first time.

I was addicted to saying *I love you.*

Or texting it.

But which heart emoji best captured the way I wanted to say *I love you* right now? I could hear Mikey clearing his throat and tapping impatiently on the boxes, but I wasn't going to let that distract me. Finding the right combination of emojis and the right heart colors was literally the most important thing in the world.

"Nick!"

Whoa. Since when did Mikey's voice get so loud and...controlling?

"Just a sec. You get started, Mikey," I said, my fingers scrolling madly through a seemingly never-ending maze of yellow faces and hearts. I'd been staring at my phone for so long they were all starting to blur.

"Oh, sure, let me just move you in all by myself then, shall I?" Mikey huffed. But out of the corner of my eye, I saw him picking up a box and taking it inside. Good boy.

"I need to take it easy. Doctor's orders, remember?" I threw that in to allay the teensy bit of guilt I felt.

I should have helped, but I just needed to...aah, there it was. Pink love heart tilted slightly on an angle with a few sparkly stars around it. Perfect! That was *exactly* how I felt right now.

Love was seriously the best thing ever. Better than anything I ever saw in movies, or read in books, or saw in movies that were based on books. Even better than any mid-'90s Mariah Carey love song.

It made me do weird things. Like hum. I'd never hummed in my entire life and now I was randomly humming all the time. Good thing I had such spectacular taste in music, but I had been humming so much, I'd gone through almost all of Christina Aguilera's back catalogue in under a week.

Love also made me skip. Okay, maybe that wasn't an entirely new thing for me, but it was the first time I had skipped when there wasn't the promise of free coffee or alcohol. Instead of just walking from, say, the bathroom to the bedroom like a normal person, somewhere along the way, my feet would lift off the ground and I found myself in mid-air.

Love was making me do all sorts of wacky things, but I loved it. I loved all of it. I loved love and I loved to love Steel Crawford.

Wait, was that a song? 'Cause that was kinda catchy. Maybe I should look into adding songwriting to my list of gigs. Couldn't be that hard, could it?

Maybe I had actually been in love with Steel for a little longer than I'd realized, because what I was feeling didn't feel entirely brand new. What was new was that I was allowing myself to feel it, allowing myself to say the words to him or text them to him, like a million times a day, now that he had gone back to work in the office.

I slung my phone into my back pocket with a self-satisfied smile, grabbed a box from the top of the pile, and followed Mikey into Steel's apartment.

"Where does this one go?" Mikey asked as he rested the box on the white marble countertop.

"What does it say on the label?"

"Miscellaneous."

Hmm...I had a lot of miscellaneous boxes because over the years, I had accumulated a lot of miscellaneous stuff. Like, you know, sparkling pink feather boas, platform shoes that were two sizes too small, and a random collection of Kylie Minogue cassette tapes from the '80s. (I didn't own a cassette player and I wasn't even born in the '80s—how did I end up with that?) It made labelling things a little interesting.

Hmm...labels. They were intriguing things indeed.

"I don't know, Mikey," I said, looking at what was scrawled on the box. "Let's leave it at the end of the hallway. I think there's a spare bedroom down there."

"You think?" Mikey quirked an eyebrow.

"I'm not sure," I replied. "For some reason, Steel keeps that room locked and it's the only room we haven't fucked in—I mean, the only room I haven't seen, yet."

"Oh my god, Nick Macklin." Mikey said the words slowly, timing them perfectly with each step he was taking closer to me. "You guys have fucked in every room? This place is like a mansion in the sky. It's huge."

"Yeah, well, it's just simple math, Mikey. I've been here, post-doctor's clearance, for eight days. There are five bedrooms, three and a half bathrooms, a kitchen, living room, dining room, and two outdoor balconies...are you adding all this up?"

Mikey smiled and pretended to be punching in the numbers on a massive, invisible calculator.

"So when I add it all up, it comes to a grand total of..." He paused for dramatic effect. He'd learned that from me. "You guys are fucking a lot."

I let out a hearty laugh. If only he knew how much—I didn't think the poor guy could handle it.

"Can you blame him, Mikey? I mean, look at this," I said, giving him a little shimmy and shake. "What man in his right mind could possibly resist all of this good stuff?"

I looked over at Mikey and he wasn't smiling at my *silly slash totally sexily awesome* dancing. In fact, his eyes looked like they were welling up with tears. He closed the distance between us and threw his arms around me. I squeezed him back just as hard.

"I love you, Nick," he said into the side of my head.

"I love you too, Mikey," I said, pulling myself away from him. "What's wrong?"

"Nothing's wrong," he said, dabbing at the edges of his eyes. "I just think you're amazing. It's so inspiring to me how confident you are with your body. And that finally, finally, *finally*, after all of these years of us being best friends, it's starting to rub off on me a little, too. I'm starting to feel more confident and it's because of you."

"Awww, Mikey." I pulled him in for another bear hug. "It's not because of me, it's because of you. You've always been strong and confident and amazing. Everyone in the world could see it, and now you can, too. I'm so happy for you."

A warmth filled my chest as I took in the sight of my best friend, brimming with his newfound confidence. He was always there by my side, through thick and thin, never wavering in his support of whatever crazy shenanigans I was getting up to.

I loved him, and I loved the *way* that I loved him. It was so different to the feelings that I had for Steel, but the cool thing was, I didn't have to choose. I could have both, and that was the best feeling in the world. Everything was coming up love!

"Alright, you can keep telling me how amazing I am, but let's get these boxes moved out of the entry, okay? Because I need some caffeine. Stat."

"Alright, let's do it," Mikey said, giving his eyes one final quick brush with the back of his hand.

I didn't actually have that many boxes, so we made light work of it.

"How do you like your coffee?" Mikey asked me once we were done moving the boxes to the end of the hallway, right outside the mystery room. We were back in the kitchen and he was staring at the scary-looking silver coffee machine with the unpronounceable European name.

"Mikey," I said, placing my palms on the white marble countertop. "I like my coffee like I like my men...hot and inside of me."

"Oh, brother." He let out a simultaneous groan and eye roll. He turned his attention back to the machine and with a few clicks, got it to make a percolating sound. "There," he said as he opened the lid and began to pour some milk into it. "I think I know what I'm doing, but I'm not entirely sure."

Ha. Words that could so easily be applied to my life.

As much as I was enjoying the high that I was on, I couldn't help but feel niggling bits of worry nipping at my feet. There was still so much that Steel and I didn't know about each other. Like what the heck was in the locked room at the end of the hallway. When I had asked Steel about it, he blushed and abruptly changed the topic to something else—kissing me.

Not that I ever minded that. The man was a seriously good kisser. And, in fact, the ways he used his talented tongue weren't just limited to my mouth. The way he worked my hole over with it, lapping and lashing away at it with such ferocity, I was surprised his jaw didn't fall off his face. It made me twitch just thinking about it.

"What are you doing?" Mikey asked with a confused look on his face. "I thought it was the coffee machine, but it's you. You're making a weird noise."

Oh shit, I was humming again.

"Nothing," I said, straightening myself on the stool. "I was just...clearing my throat."

"Hmfp." I knew that *hmfp*. "Clearing your throat to the tune of *Genie in a Bottle?*"

"I can't help it if my bodily sounds are melodic, Mikey. Now where's my damn coffee?"

"Alright, alright. Just give me a sec," he said as he turned to fiddle with the coffee machine some more while my mind returned to the one thing that I was trying to avoid thinking about.

It's funny how Mikey admired me for my confidence with my body, when secretly, it was me who was now admiring him. His strength and his ability to overcome his inner doubts and open up to his Daddy—now *that* was inspiring.

We were both boys. We both liked older men. But Mikey was more than just a boy, he was a submissive boy. He wanted to please his Daddy, and one of the ways he did that was by surrendering control. It was something very special and powerful, a connection that deepened and strengthened the love between him and Stirling tenfold.

I had something like that, too. Not the same thing, but along the same lines. Feelings that had been brewing inside of me for a long time. Thoughts and desires that had begun to bubble up to the surface and that I had been exploring online. But the internet can only take you so far.

Mikey handed me a hot cup of joe and we made our way over to the plush sofa.

"What is it? You're thinking about something..." Mikey's voice trailed off.

I always liked how he did that. He would say something to let me know that he knew something was up, but he never pushed or prodded. I gently blew into my mug, my breath mingling with the hot steam.

I gingerly took a sip before coming out with it.

"How did you know you were submissive?"

Mikey looked like he had a frog caught in his throat. He pulled the mug away from his mouth.

"Jesus, Nick, give me some warning," he said, breathing heavily. "I'm freaking out enough about sitting on a white leather sofa. I don't need you adding to it."

It was nice seeing Mikey becoming more confident, but there was also something comforting in knowing that it wasn't at the expense of his adorable clumsiness.

"Sorry, you're right. I should have given you a warning."

He reached for the stack of coasters on the coffee table, took one, and carefully placed his mug on it. He shuffled back into the sofa and crossed his legs as he looked at me. His face was neutral, but friendly.

"Where did this come from?" he asked softly.

I let out a deep breath.

"I... I've been... I just think... I mean..."

"Nick," Mikey said firmly. "Take a minute. Take as much time as you need. I'm here. I'm listening, whenever you're ready."

I nodded appreciatively. Why was this so hard? I could gyrate my ass on a podium in front of a packed nightclub. I could run an erotic cake-sitting scene like a boss at Revolver. But sitting here in front of my best friend in the world, suddenly I was feeling nervous and self-conscious. My skin felt heavy, clammy.

"I think I might be into something," I said with as much

conviction as I could muster when I finally spoke. "I just don't know if I am, because I've never done it before. So I'm confused. How can I think I like something if I've never done it before?"

There. I'd done it. I'd gotten it out.

"Well, for me," Mikey began, taking his time and being uncharacteristically deliberate with every word, "it started in much the same way as what you're going through right now. It was a feeling. Nothing more, nothing less."

I nodded my head as he continued talking.

"And then I went online and looked around a bit. I found that there were other people who were like me. But just be careful, you can go down some very weird kinky rabbit holes on the internet."

"Tell me about it," I said, taking a sip of my coffee. "I think I've been down a few of those already."

I was beginning to relax a little.

He smiled knowingly.

"But then what, Mikey?" I asked. "How do you know that what you're feeling is something that you want to actually do?"

"Well, that's the tricky part. For me, there were a couple of things I saw that I knew just weren't for me."

"Hard limits," I said, and he nodded.

"Yep, just stuff that I wasn't into. It's not a judgment on any of that, or the people who are into that sort of stuff. I just knew it wasn't a right fit for me, you know?" He leaned in a little closer. "But if you want to know if what you're feeling is something that you actually do like, Nick..."

I nodded like a maniac. Yes, yes I did. I wanted to know more than anything in the world.

Mikey blinked his big blue eyes at me. "Well, there's only one way to figure that out."

"What? How? Tell me." I was dying for him to tell me.

"You have to try it for yourself."

Oh. *Fuck.*

CHAPTER EIGHTEEN

STEEL

"Is a secret worse than a lie?" I asked Porter with a heavy sigh.

The man rolled his eyes, or at least I thought he did, I couldn't quite tell. He downed the final swig of whiskey and looked at me, the pity written across his face. That much I could tell, even in the terrible lighting.

"This place is too fucking dark," he announced grumpily. "I'm sitting right next to you, Steel, and I can barely see you. Wait, can you see me? Oh shit, am I going blind?"

I chuckled.

"Well, maybe it's true what they say, endless jacking off does make you go blind." No laughter. Not even a smile, as far as I could tell. I couldn't be entirely sure in the dark, either. "It is dark in here," I conceded.

"Good, glad it's not just me then. And for your information, I do not jack off endlessly. Well, at least, not by myself. I very rarely have to resort to that. I prefer sex that involves another person."

"No, really?" I said, half-mockingly. "That's definitely news to me." A light punch landed just under my shoulder. "Ow, quit it, Porter."

"Let's go over to the bar," he said. "It's not too busy and at least it's well lit. I might be able to actually see what I'm punching, not that I'm sure I want to."

"Let's do it," I said, getting up and crossing the not-too-busy, somewhat sticky, floor.

"We seriously need to find a cool new hangout again. This endless bar-hopping in shitty bars is getting depressing," he said, sitting down on a stool and ordering another round of drinks with a nod to the bartender. "I miss The Laird."

"I do, too," I grumbled. "But you know we can't go back there."

"I know, I know, dickass...we just need to find a better place. I mean, my standards aren't too high, are they?" I chuckled and opened my mouth to reply when he cut me off. "Don't say anything," he said, pointing a finger in my face. "God, I almost walked straight into that one, didn't I?"

I smiled and looked around the bar. It was brown and bland, lined with a wall of bottles. Luckily, there weren't too many patrons.

I had been kind of hoping for a little more privacy, but this would have to do. I had also been hoping for Stirling and Hudson to be here, but they'd both bailed at the last minute. Hudson had something come up at the gym and Stirling had Mikey, who probably came all over him. Seriously, the man almost never left the house anymore.

So it was just me and Porter for the evening, which was kind of nice. Stirling was my best friend, but Porter and Hudson weren't far behind. All three men were like brothers to me, and having some one-on-one time with each of them individually was nice every once in a while.

Stirling and Hudson tended to open up a bit more when I was with them individually. Porter, on the other hand, didn't need any more encouragement in that area. Whether it was just him and me or a crowd of a hundred, nothing could keep Porter from telling a good sex story. Or even a lousy one. It didn't seem to matter.

"Thanks," Porter smiled as the bartender slid our drinks across to us. "So, care to fill me in on what's got you asking all sorts of existential questions on a Tuesday evening?"

His lips rose into a slight smirk.

I let out a sigh before telling Porter the secret that I had been carrying for the last three weeks.

The secret that was weighing me down from the inside and filling me with a low-level dread from which I was never able to get a break.

The secret I had been keeping from Nick, somehow never able to find the right time to tell him.

Okay, that part wasn't entirely true. There had been plenty of times when I could have told him, I just didn't want to. I was enjoying being with him so much that I didn't want to do anything to ruin it.

For the first time in forever, I was with someone who made me laugh, made me terrible coffee every morning while swearing loudly at the coffee machine which he swore had a personal vendetta against him, made me kiss him first thing when I got back home in the evenings, and made me want to make the sweetest, tenderest love to him every night, over and over and over again.

And the aftercare, holy fuck, the aftercare. Whether we made love gently or fucked like two horny rabbits, it never ceased to amaze me how much Nick changed after sex. The way he became soft and mellow, needing me to look after him.

I would always do anything for him, but in those moments after sex, my desire to look after him and protect him was like a raging firestorm. It was the only thing I could see, feel, and think about. I was so deeply connected to his every movement, to his every word.

How could I ever go back to a life without any of that? The thought pressed down heavily behind my eyes. I blinked quickly a few times. A Daddy crying at a bar was not the look I was going for tonight.

"Yikes," Porter said with a pained look once I had told him the full story. "That is a dill of a pickle you've got yourself into, my friend."

"I know," I said glumly. I pushed my drink away. Alcohol wasn't going to help here. I needed to be clear-headed to think about this.

My phone vibrated and I fished it out of my pocket. A deep rush of heat settled in my chest as I saw my screen light up with hearts of every single color.

"He's quite the wordsmith," Porter said with a wry grin as he nodded at the screen.

"He's very expressive, yes," I said, before typing away a quick *I love you too* with a goofy grin on my face. God, how I would miss his constant texting if he ever left. *When* he left.

Of course he would leave. I mean, why on earth would he stay? He would blame me for the loss of his grandparents' bakery. While being technically correct, it was also technically motherfuckingly unfair.

"And things are going well, otherwise?" Porter asked.

He was trying to act innocent, but the man was fishing for details. Sex details. It was Porter, after all. He was a lot of things, but innocent wasn't one of them.

I reached for my drink. I might just need it after all.

"Yeah, things are good. Better than good, actually," I said.

"That's so good to hear. Early stage relationship sex is the best...or so I've heard." There was an undercurrent of sadness at the end of his words as he gazed down wistfully into his drink.

Porter was a sex machine, not a love machine. Long-term relationships just weren't his thing. He blamed his high-profile job as the mayor's chief of staff for not being able to settle down, but that was a bullshit excuse and we all knew it. He did, too.

No, he needed a couple of guys on the go at any given time. The name of the game wasn't love, it was not having to jack off alone. Part of me wondered whether he ever got tired of it. Sure, there was a thrill in the chase, but didn't everyone want to settle down at some point?

At least I had found someone I wanted to settle down with. Even if it was destined to come to an all-too-quick end. Was it better to have loved and lost and all that bullshit?

God, there really was no other way out of this, was there? There was no way I could pay someone to fix this or make this problem magically go away. Money was good to have, and I had worked damn hard for it, but it was useless in times like these. I could possibly shower him with gifts, maybe that would soften the blow a little? Deep down I knew it wouldn't work. Nick wasn't that kind of boy.

He'd said it himself. His favorite times were when it was just him and me. What we were doing didn't matter, nor did the expensiveness of the sofa or the impressiveness of the view from the window, all he cared about was being with me.

And I felt the same way. The swelling behind my eyes had returned, more forcefully this time. I bit down on my lower lip, determined not to completely lose my shit in public.

"So I've come up with two new acronyms," Porter said excitedly, in a blatant attempt to lighten the dark clouds that had gathered above me. "Patent pending, of course, and they're pretty damn good. You wanna hear 'em?"

I looked at him and couldn't help but smile. He was like a child wanting his parents' approval, yelling for them to look at him as he dove into the pool.

"Sure," I said with a nod. "Let me hear what you got."

"Okay," he said, drumming his fingers on the table. "The first one. BOY. The Porter Jones next-level acronym is: Brash. Obedient. Young."

"Hmm...not bad," I said. "A little Dom-y, but yeah, okay."

"Not bad?" Porter looked at me like I had just spat in his face. "It's incredible. Okay, this one will knock your socks off, Steel."

More drum rolling on the table.

"BRAT. The Porter Jones next-level acronym for that is: Boy who'd Rather Attract Trouble."

I couldn't help laugh at his sheer idiocy.

"You're so silly sometimes," I said, shaking my head at him. He was a grown man, after all.

"Hey, it made you smile," he replied and there was a genuine warmth in his eyes. His face grew serious as he spoke again, "Things aren't that bad, Steel. Look, you know you have to tell him, so tell him. Sure, Nick might be upset with you for a little while, but you guys can deal with it. Every relationship goes through its ups and downs. This will just be one of those downs, that's all."

And what a major downer it was going to be. I didn't know what would happen. Would he leave me? I was hoping with every fiber of my being that he wouldn't, but I had to brace myself for it. It was more than likely that he would.

But could he? Could he actually walk away from what we had? From me?

I knew I had no other choice. Whatever happened would be something I would have to deal with one way or another.

I had to tell Nick the truth.

CHAPTER NINETEEN

NICK

I think it's time for a little montage. I love a good movie montage once in a while. Spoiler—I also just love saying the word *montage*. It makes me feel so...French.

So in the montage from this last week, here's what would be included.

Cut to: Me. I was born for penthouse living. Every room in the apartment was huge and there was just so much space everywhere. Space that I was happy to fill up.

In addition to humming and skipping, I'd also added spontaneous dancing to my repertoire. Because sometimes life was just so damn good that a boy couldn't help but *bust a move*. (Hmm, I might add that one to my songwriting lyrics notepad too, that could be super catchy).

Or strut a move. I mean, the long hallways were practically as wide as runways. And I had been doing a lot of my second-favorite thing in the world: thrift store shopping, so I had plenty of new outfits to show off and strut about in front of Steel.

He loved it, too. His light blue eyes would sparkle as I paraded around for him, rocking my hips, shaking my meaty ass with whatever cute little piece I had snagged for a bargain-basement price. I had a sneaking suspicion it was his second-favorite thing in the world too.

Cut to: Our number one most favoritest thing in the world—sex!

I mean, the man had a voracious appetite that showed no signs of slowing down. Sometimes, once a night wasn't enough for him. His recovery time needed to be investigated by the Guinness Book of Records—or by scientists—because it was seriously impressive. Men half his age would be jealous. Which was fine with me. My body was an all-you-can-eat buffet and I was open for the man twenty-four-seven.

In just the past few nights, he had taken me on the marble kitchen countertop, twice in the shower, and once up against the floor-to-ceiling windows in the lounge, which was not only super exiting because it felt like all of Daylseford could see us, but was also super hot because I could see his face in the reflection as he pounded against me with all his might.

I even gave the man a blowjob on the private rooftop terrace. The cool night air grazed my face as he throatfucked me with his blazing hot cock, filling me with his delicious cum and leaving my lips the kind of swollen that would cost a couple of hundred bucks to get at the beautician's.

Then there'd be a cut to a close-up of our faces after sex. Okay, that was my number one most favoritest, *favoritest* thing in the world. Those moments after sex—or aftercare, as he called it— when something changed in Steel.

He was always caring and considerate, but after we'd had sex, it was like he took it to a whole other level. Our bodies had been so connected and in tune with each other, and afterward, his every word, his every breath was intermingled with mine. His focus was solely on me and making sure I was alright. It was blissful, like lying on a big, white, fluffy cloud.

Cut to: Present moment.

Steel's face was scanning the thousand puzzle pieces strewn across on the coffee table in front of us. I looked amazing in cute gray sweatpants and a black-and-gold top I had op-shopped that week, even though I was a little miffed that I had spilled ice cream on myself earlier that night.

"I'm looking for a window," he said in an adorably serious tone.

I giggled. "You're too cute, you know that?"

"What?" He looked up at me, all wide-eyed and charmingly cute.

The man had an endless supply of white t-shirts which made his muscles bulge in all sorts of sexy ways every time he moved. I couldn't resist the urge to reach over and plant a kiss on his forehead.

"I love that you love this," I said, pointing at the puzzle we had just unwrapped. "And I love that we're doing this together."

"Of course, baby, I love spending time with you, too. I'm just glad we've moved on from—"

"Britney, Whitney, Shania, Mariah?" I asked.

If a pop diva had a puzzle, there was a good chance we had already done it. Maybe that's where the money in music was these days? Who knew?

His eyes crinkled in a warm smile. "Yeah, I mean nothing against any of them, they're all great."

"Legendary," I corrected.

"Right..." he smiled as he continued, "...but there's something about seeing a half-put-together human face on a puzzle that is just freaky."

I could see that. Although I personally thought that seeing a half-put-together exposed belly was freakier, hence why my puzzle strategy always involved starting at the belly button.

"Is that why you chose this....what is this, actually?"

I looked over at the puzzle box and frowned. The dreary-looking, diva-less puzzle box.

"It's Windsor castle," Steel replied.

We had done the last four puzzles that I had wanted to do, so it was his turn to choose. Ooh, look at me compromising. See? Adulting ain't that hard.

"Maybe that's why you can't find the window piece. There's like a million windows on this thing. It's going to take us forever to finish."

A look flashed across Steel's face and disappeared just as quickly, before I had a chance to figure out what it was.

"Maybe that's why I chose it, so we get to be together forever," he said.

Our eyes met and my heart fluttered as it always did whenever he spoke to me and looked at me like that...but something was a little off. Steel had a jittery nervousness about him that just wasn't like him.

He'd been that way ever since he had caught up with Porter last week. And when we weren't fucking, doing puzzles, or putting on mini fashion shows, the *slightly off* feeling would always come back. It was there just under the surface of his words, just that little bit too far away for me to put my finger on and ask him about.

It was like he wanted to tell me something, but for some reason couldn't. I looked over at him and he was doing another weird thing that he'd only just started doing last week. Every once in a while, he would glance over at me, super quickly so that I almost didn't catch it, and look at my fingers. That was it. Why was the man suddenly so obsessed with my fingers when there were so many other awesome parts of my body he could be captivated by?

Even when we were having sex, he would interlace his fingers into mine and kiss them. After sex, he would do the same, constantly peppering my fingers with little kisses.

And then it hit me, the lightbulb going off in my head. The

lightbulb shattering as my brain finally put all the pieces—pun intended—together.

Him looking like he had something to say but was too nervous to say it.

His sudden obsession with my fingers, staring at them as if he were studying them...maybe, measuring them in his mind?

Holy mother of Beyoncé, Steel Crawford was going to propose to me.

"You okay, baby?" Steel asked, looking up at me. "Your fingers just started shaking."

Again with the finger-watching. I reached for the glass of water with my increasingly shaky fingers.

"I might just..." I gulped the whole glass right down. "I might just get some fresh air."

"Oh, great. I'll come with you."

"Great."

Years of practicing fake smiling in front of the mirror, as if I had lost the Grammy Award but knew the camera was still on me, were really paying off right now.

Being the gentleman that he always was, Steel walked ahead and slid the massive glass door wide, holding it open for me.

"Thanks," I said, walking past him. Trying not to look at him. Trying not to breathe him in the way I always did.

I strode over to the edge and let out a massive breath as I gripped the cold bricks. The night air hit my face, reminding me of the last time we were out here. Me on my knees in front of him with something else of his hitting me in the face...

"Are you okay?" Steel asked, pulling up beside me, gently touching my lower back. "I know a castle isn't as exciting as—"

"It's not that," I said, turning to face him.

His face was lit up by a thousand city lights. His thick silver hair was slightly messed up from the thousand times I had kissed him and run my fingers through it that night. My body was trembling at the thousand crazy thoughts racing through my mind in a whirlwind of confusion and exhilaration.

I looked down at my still shaky fingers and then back at him. God, could I do it? Could I actually marry the man? I had thought our night would end with Steel coming inside of me and me falling asleep wrapped up in his arms like always. This was the last thing I had been expecting.

I hadn't really ever given marriage a serious thought. Before Steel, my longest serious relationship had been a threesome with two guys named Ben & Jerry (who came in a wonderful assortment of flavors). I was only twenty-four, was I even the marrying kind? The kind of guy that wanted to settle down and be a...husband? Maybe even one day have...kids?

And what the hell would I wear for the wedding? Was white appropriate or, like, so twentieth century? Would we wear matching tuxedos or go individual? Would the Destiny's Child cover band be available? There was so much to think about.

"I'm actually glad we're out here, Nick."

Steel's words snapped me back to reality. My *I'm about to be proposed to* reality that I hadn't spent any time in the mirror preparing for. I was going to have to wing my reaction face.

"I have to tell you something."

Oh god, he was going to do it. He was going to propose to me and I was wearing sweatpants and an ice-cream-stained t-shirt. Okay, I could make this work. If I tied the shirt up into a knot, it would cover the stain and as a bonus, expose my belly that he loved so much. There was hardly any time to think, it was all happening so fast.

My heart was beating so hard, but I did my best to play it cool.

"Oh sure," I said with a casual hair flick and forcing a casual...ly petrified smile across my lips.

This was so major and I was so not ready. I didn't even have my cell phone to take a selfie for after I said...yes?

But then I looked into Steel's eyes and all of my mind's

ramblings disappeared like smoke into thin air. The man loved me. The man looked after me. We lived together. We got on so well together. Maybe we could spend the rest of our lives together?

"My firm is representing the developers who want to take your grandparents' bakery." The words filled the air like stench coming from a sewage plant.

"What?"

I couldn't have heard that right, but he wasn't down on his knees with an open jewelry box, and he wasn't looking up at me with the adoration of someone who wanted to spend a lifetime with me.

No. He just stood there looking every inch the cold, deceitful, asshole lawyer that he'd always said he didn't want to be.

But that was classic Steel. Say one thing, do something else.

"Are you serious?" I sputtered in disbelief. "How—how is this even possible?"

"Let me explain," he reached out to touch my forearm, but I pulled it away from him.

The anger was rising in me and I wanted to have my hands clenched into fists by my side for what he was about to say.

What the hell could he even say? He was destroying two people's lives. Two people that I loved and cared about so much. Two people who had put their lives on hold to raise me. Two people that he had been so nervous about meeting and wanting to impress.

But all of that was bullshit. Just like his whole *I'm a totally self-made man* story was bullshit too. Steel Crawford was a lot of things, but self-made was not one of them.

He started talking, but I couldn't listen to the lies falling out of his mouth. My head was pounding with rage and drowning everything else out. The bits and pieces I heard only made me madder.

"We only work with good people, they have great plans for that space..."

"They've made your grandparents a very, very generous offer...."

"I had no idea they were the same developers until we had dinner with your grandparents..."

"Wait, you've known about it since *then*?" I snapped and his expression turned to one of guilt. Pure, icy-cold guilt.

"All this time, Steel, you've known and you didn't tell me. Worse...you haven't done a single damn thing to stop it, have you?"

"I can't stop it, Nick. That's not how it works. Even if my firm walked away from the developers and refused to help them, another firm would represent them. It's a done deal, Nick. I'm really sorry that it affects your grandparents like this, but there's nothing I can do. I've done everything in my power to ensure that all parties are compensated fairly..."

"Spare me your bullshit, Steel. What would you know about being compensated fairly?"

"What's that supposed to mean?" The shock in his voice pummeled my chest, but I forced myself to push through it.

"You're not a self-made man, Steel, are you? You're a trust fund baby. You come from money. You've always had money. You have no idea what it's like not to have it. So you can take your fair compensation...and shove it up your ass."

Steel's eyes were racing across my face and his chest was heaving. This was our first fight and he was clearly losing.

Not much of a lawyer.

Not much of a boyfriend.

And definitely not much of a future fiancé.

"How did you know...about the trust fund?" he asked, staring at the ground. The man I'd thought I loved couldn't even look me in the eye.

"I stalked you online after we first met. There was an article in *The Daylesford Times* from years ago. That's where I read it."

"So, that's why you didn't like me. I mean, there was the thing that you overheard me saying on the yacht, and then this as well, right?"

"That's right," I replied sharply. "So, is it true? About the trust fund then?" I knew it was, but I just wanted to see whether he would continue lying to me.

"It is," he said, looking up. His eyes were glazed with tears. "But it's not what you think, Nick."

"You don't know what I think, Steel," I snapped back. "Because if you did know me even a little, you'd know how unforgivable this is. And the fact that you've kept this from me all this time..."

I shook my head at him as I started to walk away.

"I'm outta here first thing tomorrow morning," I said. "And I'm paying you back for everything you've ever paid for."

And with those words, I went back inside, ran into the bathroom, and slammed the door shut. I fell to the floor, my body bracing against the cold tiles, my mind spinning in a montage reel from hell. It was like one of those times when your whole life flashed before your eyes, my whole relationship with Steel was flashing before mine.

Everything.

All of it.

From the first time we met when Mikey and I were naked butlers at his fortieth, to all the times he'd tried to make a move but I'd cut him down afterward, to how he'd showed up at The Tank Top and for the first time, we'd talked. Like, properly talked.

To the time he broke my ass when we were having sex and I ended up moving in here. To all the times when we'd spent hours on the floor by the coffee table doing puzzles and just chatting away, simply enjoying each other's company.

To me being the biggest idiot in the world and thinking the man would actually propose to me tonight. I slid down the cold, hard tiles until I was lying on the cold, hard floor, looking up at the bright yellow lights.

It was over.

All of it.

Everything.

CHAPTER TWENTY

STEEL

"Shit, shit, shit."

"Porter," Hudson growled. "Stop it. That's not helping."

That was the depressing thing. Nothing could help. Nothing could make this better. I was powerless, and I hated being powerless.

I looked around at Porter, Hudson, and Stirling as we sat around in Porter's sunken living room. The same living room where I had met Nick for the very first time at my fortieth. It felt like a lifetime ago. My heart clenched at the memory. My friends' faces were almost as glum as mine.

"Need more beer," I said to Porter, raising my nearly empty glass.

"Coming right up," Porter said, getting to his feet. "Can I get anyone else anything?" A look of mock horror swept across his face as he did a double take. "Oh good god, has it really come to this?

Hanging out at my place because we can't find a good bar? *Me* being *your* server?"

"Sounds like one of your scenes at Revolver," Hudson joked, and I smiled, appreciating the big guy's attempt to lighten the mood.

"More like a nightmare," Porter muttered as he left the room.

A few moments later, he returned with a six-pack of beer under one arm, and a cooler in the other. He handed me a bottle, and put the remaining bottles into the cooler.

"What's all this?" Stirling asked him.

"I'm not getting up again. I don't serve Daddies," Porter said all huffily and puffily as he sat back down and folded his arms in front of his chest. "I get served by boys."

"Well, there you go," Hudson said, throwing a *Porter is in one of his moods* glance at Stirling and me.

The good thing about having friends that you've known for twenty years is that you can just be yourself with them. Good, bad, or ugly, it doesn't matter. We had seen each other through it all and we always had each other's backs, even if it meant that we weren't always perky and happy, or if we sometimes irritated the shit out of each other. We were brothers, family, and I knew deep in my heart that nothing would ever change that.

Porter was frustrated that we couldn't find a cool new hangout, most likely because it deprived him of a place to pick up guys. He was probably horny, and since jacking off was beneath him, he was undoubtedly suffering an almighty case of blue balls. Hence his current surly mood. And that was fine.

Stirling was still all loved up and honeymoon-y with Mikey. Stirling's presence at this gathering was a rare occurrence since I felt like we hardly got to see him anymore, but that was okay. I knew he'd resurface eventually and I wanted him to enjoy this experience with Mikey. Even if it meant that he was wearing a god-awful ugly cardigan, trying—and failing—to cover up the hickeys all over his neck. He kept tugging at it, constantly pulling it up toward his face. And that was fine.

Hudson was having work stress with his three gyms. He was struggling to find new members. Apparently a number of new gyms had opened in Daylesford and gym goers were fickle, going wherever the latest fitness trend took them, causing a massive issue for Hudson's bottom line. He looked tired, stressed, and distracted. And that was fine too.

Life wasn't perfect and didn't always go according to plan. At least we had each other and could be our true pissed-off, stressed-out selves in front of one another.

I checked my phone and winced as I read the email confirming that the deal had just gone through. It was signed, sealed, and delivered. The developer had signed on the dotted line. Nick's grandparents' bakery was no more...and neither were we. I let out a heavy, depressed sigh into my beer.

"So what are you going to do?" Stirling asked, his green eyes filled with worry.

I rubbed my face in frustration. "Nothing, Stirling. There is absolutely nothing I can do here. That's what I've spent the last week trying to get through to Nick. This is all out of my hands."

"And let me guess, he wasn't open to it?" Porter asked in a low voice.

"That's putting it mildly," I said.

It killed me that there was nothing I could do to fix this problem and make Nick feel better. I wasn't used to feeling like this. So fucking powerless.

Normally, every problem I encountered was solvable. That didn't mean that there was an easy solution or a quick fix, but I always managed to find a way to overcome whatever was placed in front of me. I wasn't the kind of man who was afraid of rolling up his sleeves and putting in the hard work.

In spite of what Nick knew about my background. Or thought he knew.

"And what about the trust fund stuff?" Hudson asked me. "Are you going to tell him?"

"You have to tell him," Porter answered for me before I could. "You are not a trust fund baby, Steel. At least not in the bad, entitled, spoiled, rich-kid way. He needs to know that."

"Does he?" I said with a scoff. "What difference would it even make at this point?"

"Hey, hey, hey," Stirling said as he got up off his chair and moved over to the couch I was sitting on. He placed his hand on my knee and said, "Don't give up on this, Steel. You guys have a good thing going."

"Had," I said, raising my finger in the air. "*Had* a good thing going. I think we're technically broken up at this point."

"Technically-shmechnically," Porter said. "You're actually not broken up because neither one of you said the words, right?"

I looked around the room and the guys nodded their agreement.

"Great, so my relationship is hanging on by a thread. A technical thread. I hate feeling like this, you guys. It really sucks."

I sulked my way deeper into the couch, settling against the firm back. Should I tell Nick about the trust fund? I mean, he really only had half of the story. Maybe if he knew the other half, it would change things. The glimmer of hope that rose in my chest at the thought felt out of place.

No, Nick was stubborn and it would take more than me explaining things about my financial situation to get him to change his mind and come back to me. There wasn't much hope to cling to. There wasn't much of *anything* to cling to. Nick was gone.

How I wanted him to come back to me.

The last week without him had been truly awful. I hadn't slept. I hadn't eaten. I hadn't been in the office all week and I hadn't shaved. I was one mess of a Daddy—and I knew it. I dragged my fingers across my stubbled jaw and let out an exasperated sigh.

The apartment was eerily quiet without Nick in it. I felt like a zombie, mindlessly wandering from room to room in the middle of the day, still in my pajamas, with nothing on my mind but him. On a good day, I'd shower by four and maybe take a stab at eating some takeout. On a good day...

My phone suddenly vibrated and I fished it out of my pants.

It was Nick.

My stomach dropped to the floor. I knew this wouldn't be good. The guys could tell by my face who it was and they all fell silent as I read his text out.

"He's found out about the deal," I said, looking up at them briefly. My throat felt like someone had wrapped their fingers around it and was strangling me, slowly and painfully.

My eyes scanned the rest of the text.

"And yep, he's broken up with me...how could I do this to him? Did I ever even love him? I've destroyed his grandparents' lives...and his."

I looked up at my friends and was *this close* to completely losing my shit and bursting into tears.

"Oh man, I'm so sorry," Hudson said, leading the chorus of condolences.

"Well, at least now I know where we stand. Technically."

Porter grimaced. "It still sucks, Steel. And it's unfair. He doesn't know the full story and he's upset because they're his grandparents, you know? They raised him, so obviously it's going to hurt him if they're hurting."

"I know," I said, looking around the room, trying to avoid the pitying looks that were being directed at me.

I did know, but it didn't make it any easier. All the rationalization and logic in the world wouldn't make an iota of difference. My chest felt like it was being squeezed, making it hard to even breathe.

I had lost the only boy I had ever loved.

I closed my eyes as I felt my heart break into a million pieces.

This was one puzzle I wasn't ever going to be able to put back together.

CHAPTER TWENTY-ONE

NICK

"Gramps, what are you doing down there?" I said, peering down into the dimly lit basement. I'd seen him go down the stairs and, a few moments later, heard a loud crashing sound. "Are you okay?"

A cold shiver swept through me as I made my way down the stairs after him. For some reason, basements always freaked me out. Maybe I'd had some traumatic childhood experience in one that I'd successfully managed to suppress for twenty-four years. Whatever it was, basements were just creepy. They were where psychopaths lived and planned their next kill.

But if Grandpa had fallen or was in any kind of trouble, I wasn't going to let anything stop me from getting down there and helping him as fast as I could.

"I'm alright, Nick," he said as I walked up behind him.

He was standing over a half-open box. My box. One of my many labeled-as- miscellaneous boxes that I had stored in my grandparents' basement after moving out of Steel's apartment and back into my grandparents' house.

"Are you sure?" I asked, looking at him carefully. He seemed a little out of breath, but otherwise fine.

"Yes, I'm alright. I just wasn't looking where I was going and I ran into this pile of boxes. I'm sorry, Nick, I think I might have broken something."

"It's fine, Gramps, don't worry about it," I said, giving his shoulder a squeeze.

It wasn't like I really had anything valuable anyway. Well, apart from my collection of cock-shaped shot glasses made out of crystals. But my life wouldn't be over if they were broken.

"I'm the one who should be saying sorry for cluttering up your basement with all of my sh...er, stuff, Gramps."

We both looked around the place. It was stacked to the brim with mountains of brown boxes, most of them at least six feet high. In Steel's apartment, it hadn't looked like much, but here, apart from a couple of narrow paths I had kept clear, there was hardly any room left to move. Which, in a way, was a good thing—it meant there wasn't any room for a serial-killing psychopath to move in here, either.

"We love having you here, Nick."

Grandpa's eyes crinkled as he smiled lovingly at me, instantly making me feel like I was right where I belonged.

But *did* I belong here?

Having a place to come back to when life throws a shitstorm in your face was always a good thing. I knew that, and I was incredibly grateful to my grandparents for taking me in after I had stupidly given up the lease on my apartment when I moved in with Steel.

But until last week, I'd thought that I belonged with Steel. I'd thought we were happy together. I'd thought we were meant to be together. I'd even thought about whether I should be the one to change my surname, or him his, if we got married. I couldn't decide what sounded better—Nick Crawford or Steel Macklin.

But now I didn't know anything.

"Thanks, Gramps," I said, wrapping my arms around the man who had been there for me my whole life. He'd been there for my first day of school. He'd come to all my recitals and athletic meets. Every Christmas, he'd always be the one dressed up as Santa, right up until when I was too old to believe in Santa (at the totally-reasonable age of thirteen). The man wasn't just my grandpa. He was my hero, too.

"You guys are the best," I said as my heart clenched.

They were the best, they really were, and my heart broke for them because they had lost their bakery. It wasn't just a business for them, it was their lifelong passion. A place they had dedicated themselves to for the last forty-five years.

Now it was all gone. They had received a thirty-day-notice to evacuate. And just like that, a lifetime of hard work and memories would vanish without a trace, as if it had never happened at all.

They were still in shock, obviously. They didn't want to talk about it too much, and I respected that. I couldn't imagine how hard it must have been for them to get the news. Especially knowing that Steel was the person behind all of it. The man they had welcomed so warmly into their home and seemed to get along so well with.

Yeah, that guy. The same guy who had, only a few short weeks later, betrayed them. Betrayed all of us. And for what? So that some greedy developer could gentrify yet another part of the city and make it feel like Anywheresville? Who cared about a few mom-and-pop businesses when there was money to be made, right?

"What were you looking for, Gramps? Why'd you come down here?" I asked.

"These," he said with a bright smile as he waved a pair of gardening gloves in his hands. "Need to do some weeding this afternoon. This is my favorite pair. I thought I'd lost them, but then your grandma remembered they were down here."

"Alright, well, speaking of Grandma, let's go upstairs. Dinner's almost ready."

I quickly picked up the box that had fallen and shoved back in all the random things that had fallen out, before following Gramps up the stairs and into the part of the house where the normal, non-psychopathic people lived.

Dinner these days was usually a pretty quiet affair, mainly consisting of Grandma and Gramps asking me about my day and me trying desperately to avoid asking about theirs, not wanting to bring up the topic of the bakery at all. My grandparents knew that I had a few jobs, but I sanitized the finer details of my working life for them a little. Okay, a lot.

They thought I worked at The Tank Top as a bartender. Which technically wasn't incorrect. I did work-slash-dance-slash-twerk my ass off on the bar most nights.

They thought I worked as an actual butler for Hunter's company. That was true. The only lie was one of omission. Me omitting the fact that I didn't wear any clothing.

They also thought that I worked as a cake courier. Yeah, that one was a bit of a stretch, I'll admit. But there was no family-friendly, PG-rated version of erotic cake-sitting that I could come up with. So it made sense to say that I knew people who wanted elaborate cakes and that I would personally deliver the cakes to them. Erotic cake-sitting was hard enough to explain to a thirty-eight-year-old, much less to my sixty-eight-year-old grandparents.

We finished the meal more quietly than usual. I hadn't noticed anything was off. I was too busy wrapped up in my own self-pitying thoughts about Steel. It wasn't until I got up to clear the table that I saw their eyes were locked on me.

"What?" I asked, reaching for their plates. "Have I got food on my face or something?"

The chair screeched behind me as I stood up.

"Nick, please sit down." There was a rare firmness in my grandmother's voice, one that was usually reserved for not-so-pleasant conversations.

I sat down slowly, eyeing them both as my ass landed in the seat and my heart started thumping a little faster in my chest.

"We need to talk," Gramps said as he cupped his palm over Grandma's delicate hand.

Oh shit. Something was wrong. Was it about their financial situation? Was I walking around the house swearing too much? Was I taking too much time to get ready in the bathroom in the morning? I mean, I could probably shave off two, maybe three minutes, but anything under a thirty-minute morning routine was completely unrealistic for me. I did *not* just wake up like this.

Was one of them sick? Oh no, were both of them sick? Panic started to rise in my chest as I darted my eyes from one to the other and then back again.

Finally, Grandma spoke. "Nick, I don't know how to say this."

"Just tell me," I said, gulping hard. "Whatever it is, Grandma, I can handle it. Just give it to me straight."

"Well, Nick," she said with a slight tilt of her head. "You're being a dick."

"Millie!" My grandpa turned and stared at his wife of almost fifty years like he was looking at a complete stranger. A complete stranger with a potty mouth.

"What?" she said with a shrug. "It's true, Ray, he is. And I know you agree with me."

What alternative world was I living in right now? Did my grandmother actually just call me a dick? Did my grandfather actually agree with her?

"Your grandmother's right," Gramps added, just in case I needed the night to get any more surreal.

I hadn't been this shocked since I figured out what Ariana Grande's 34 + 35 added up to.

"What—what...why are you guys calling me a...?" For the first time in my life, I didn't want to use a curse word in front of my grandparents.

"Steel," they both said in unison.

"There are a few things you need to know, Nick," Grandpa said as he straightened up in his seat.

"And maybe once you know them," Grandma said with a wicked twinkle in her eyes, "you'll change your mind and stop being such a..."

"Grandma! Language, please."

A smile stretched across her lips. I had never seen this sassy side of her before...and I kinda loved it. Maybe that was where I got it from?

"What?" she said, reverting back to sweet-little-grandma mode as if nothing weird had just taken place. "Once you say it one time, it is kind of fun."

"You were saying, Grandpa?" I said with a loud exhalation, turning toward the man and, for once, being the adult in the family.

"Number one," he started, not wasting a second, "Steel was helping us out financially after you had your...uh, accident."

"Wait, what?" My hand slammed down on the table involuntarily.

Grandma nodded. "He would order at least five fancy cakes from us each week."

What on earth would Steel need five cakes a week for? The image of Steel being an erotic cake-sitter flashed in my mind for the briefest moment before Grandpa, thankfully, swept it away.

"He bought them for his staff," he said.

"But we really knew he was just doing it to help us," Grandma added. "The bakery hasn't been making a profit in years, Nick."

Yeah, tell me about it.

I looked over at them both. They were smiling, clearly touched by Steel's kind gesture.

I was kind of touched by it, too. Maybe, sorta, just a smidge. It still didn't make up for the fact that the man had orchestrated my grandparents losing their bakery, but...it was a super nice thing for him to do for them. He knew how freaked out I was after the accident, when I realized that I wouldn't be able to support them.

"Number two, the bakery," Grandpa began as he took in a deep breath. "Nick, we were glad to let it go."

"Huh? But—but...that's your whole life. You've both worked so hard for so many years...I don't understand," I sputtered.

What was I hearing?

"You're right," Grandma began. "We have been working hard for a long time, Nick. And we're tired. We actually wanted to stop working."

"And with the money the developer gave us, now we can," Gramps said. A look of relief washed over his face.

"And thanks to Steel, the developer's offer was more than generous," Grandma added. Her face was relaxing too. They were both looking calm and...happy. Calmer and happier than I had seen them in a very long time.

"But what about the bakery? You guys loved that place, didn't you?"

"We did," Gramps said with a nod. "And we always will. But it's time to let it go, Nick. Nothing will change the fact that it was such a big part of our lives for so many years. Nothing will take away all the memories that we made there."

"We're just ready for a new part of our lives to begin," Grandma added softly.

"What are you saying?" I asked.

They looked at each other apprehensively, as if silently trying to figure out which one of them would be the one to say it.

Gramps finally bit the bullet and just said it. "We're going traveling, Nick."

"Traveling? At your...?"

Two thick eyebrows shot up into the air and I knew better than to finish that question if I wanted even the slightest shot at scoring some dessert tonight.

"I've always wanted to go to Paris, it's just so romantic," Grandma said, her face lighting up in dreamy delight.

"And I did one of those internet DNA test thingies," Grandpa said. "Turns out..."

My entire body tensed up, fighting against the urge to blurt out, *"turns out I'm 100% that bitch."* I didn't think my grandparents would appreciate the finer intricacies of Lizzo's amazing lyrics. Although, who knew? Grandma was throwing *dicks* around left, right, and center tonight, and Gramps was doing DNA testing online. Who were these people?

"...I have Bulgarian heritage. I wouldn't mind visiting," he said, joining Grandma in a bout of wistful gazing.

Okay, Paris, I kinda knew where that was, but Bulgaria? Was that even a real place? If it was, it sounded like it would be really far away. And cold. Definitely cold.

But I looked over at them and they just seemed so...different. Lighter, somehow. I guess I missed that the bakery, for all the joy it brought, had been quietly weighing them down. Maybe after forty-five years of carrying that burden, they deserved to let it go and just live their lives for themselves. I knew better than anyone just how much they had sacrificed for me.

Maybe I needed to wake the fuck up and get out of their way. And get out of my own stupid way, too.

"So when are you getting back together with Steel?" Grandma asked, shooting me an expectant look.

"I'm not getting back together with Steel, Grandma."

I hated how awful those words sounded coming out of my mouth. I couldn't. It was done. I had moved out. I had subjected the man to plenty of yelling and shouting. I had made it abundantly clear that things between us were over.

But god, I missed him. I missed him so much it hurt. I missed him so much, and I kept thinking about him. Like, all the time. And now I was learning all of *this* from my grandparents. My breath hitched in my throat.

Had I made the biggest mistake of my life?

Steel had helped my grandparents survive while I was out of work. He didn't have to do that, and he did it without telling me. He wasn't trying to impress me by throwing his money around, as some sort of blatant attempt to get back in my good books. No, he was doing it because he was a decent guy.

And he was right when he said that if it hadn't been his law firm representing the developers, it would have been another one. At least he did everything he could to get the best deal for my grandparents.

And it had worked. They both seemed to be his biggest cheerleaders and lifelong stans. They saw the good in him. That he was decent. How he looked after me. The connection that we...had.

In a funny way, Steel had actually given them both something that I couldn't—a new start. I hadn't even realized that was what they'd wanted. But now that I did, I wasn't going to be selfish by making it about me. They deserved, more than anyone I knew, to live their lives happily.

"I don't know what I can do," I said, letting out a deep, exasperated breath. "I broke up with Steel. I've yelled at him. I've used a lot of bad words."

"Bad words aren't always so bad," Grandma said, that mischievous twinkle returning to her eyes. "And if you broke up with that amazing man, then you should simply un-break up with him."

CHAPTER TWENTY-TWO

STEEL

"Guys, why are we doing this?" I asked as we stood waiting near the front of the line outside of the movie theater.

I was trying not to sound whiny, but it was cold out. I zipped my jacket up a little higher and rubbed my hands together.

"It'll be fun," Hudson said. He was smiling.

That was weird. Hudson wasn't a smiler.

"You realize I have a media room at home with a screen pretty much the same size, right? We could literally watch anything we want, and we wouldn't have to wait in line," I said grumpily.

"It's good to get out," Stirling said. He was smiling, too, which had lately become a more common occurrence for the man.

But I had a sneaking suspicion that his current, abnormally smiley facial expression had nothing to do with Mikey.

I wasn't a huge fan of going to the movies and the guys knew that. In the twenty years we'd known each other, we might have gone to the movies together twice, if that.

I didn't like waiting in line in the cold just to get in. I didn't like getting ripped off paying for cold popcorn and an oversized soda. And I was one of those 'shushers'. You know, one of those people who requested that completely unreasonable thing: that people simply keep their mouths shut while the movie was playing. Outrageous, right? Humans just weren't designed to sit in a darkened room with people they didn't know to watch a movie they could see at home.

"I seriously think the last time I was at the movies was in the '90s," I said to the guys. "What are we seeing, by the way?"

"*Romy and Michele's High School Reunion*," Hudson said, tapping his fingers together excitedly like a schoolkid. "It's my all-time favorite."

"Really? I had you pegged as more of a *Rambo* or *Die Hard* kinda guy," Stirling said, unable to hide the bemused look on his face.

I ignored them, returning to my original thought.

"So wait, you're telling me we're in line like it's the '90s, to see a movie literally from the '90s?"

"Yeah," Porter said with a distracted smile as he looked around the crowd. "Hollywood's officially given up. They're not even doing remakes anymore. They're just re-releasing their whole back catalog. And look around—it's popular, Steel."

I took a look around us, and he was right. The line stretched as far as I could see, snaking its way around the block. For the life of me, I couldn't understand why. Didn't people have anything better to do?

And what was wrong with my friends? I squinted at each of them, only to be met with a whole bunch of weird nodding and exaggerated word mouthing. Before I could ask them what the heck they were up to...

"Alright, guys, let's get him into position," Stirling said, and before I knew what was happening, they had pushed me to the front of the line. Music started playing. It sounded familiar. I heard the first few piano chords of...was that Fatboy Slim's *Praise You?*

I used to love that song...back in the '90s.

Right in front of the concession stand, a group of about eight people had gathered. They were standing in a line, bending over, their arms flung out to the sides, holding hands like a human chain. Behind them, I could make out a guy wearing a shirt with brown stripes, crouching on the ground.

As the words to the song started, the guy in the brown-striped shirt stood up and the row of bent-over people also got up, lifting their arms into the air. When the beat of the song kicked in, the people began dancing in time with the music, except for the guy in the striped brown shirt. He was off doing his own crazy thing. They all had their backs to us, so I couldn't see any of their faces, but it was clear what was happening here...it was a flash mob.

How very '90s.

I laughed and saw that Stirling, Porter, and Hudson weren't looking at the dancers. They were looking at me.

"You're going to like this," Stirling said with a smile.

"Like what?" I replied, and turned my head back to the dancers.

Suddenly, the song hit a crescendo and the dancers really went off, shaking and flailing their whole bodies around. Just like in the music video, which was starting to come back to me. They were recreating the flash mob by doing a flash mob. It was all very meta, but the geeky '90s kid in me loved it.

The dancer that really went off, though, was the guy in the brown-striped shirt, the one in the role of the lead dancer from the music video. When he turned around to face us, my stomach dropped to the ground.

It was Nick.

He flashed me a wide, toothy smile, before joining the dancers in a hard-to-describe jumping sort of move that had them leaping through the air like frogs. A large crowd was beginning to gather all around them, cell phones in hand, but I had the best spot, with a clear view of Nick.

Oh dear...the reverse-swimming fishy move. I remembered that from the music video and cringed. It was cringe-inducing in the '90s and it was definitely still cringe-inducing in the 2020s. Not that Nick looked like he was self-conscious in the slightest. I wasn't surprised by Nick's confidence at all.

He was the most unique person I had ever met. Truly one of a kind. The kind that didn't give a shit what anybody else thought about him. The kind that would organize a flash mob in front of a movie theater on a chilly night...just for me.

My chest expanded with joy, like a helium balloon ready to float into the sky. It also reassured me that I'd made the right decision earlier that day. I couldn't wait to tell him.

But first, back to the song.

The running airplane—a classic move. Nick's face was getting sweaty, so it was a good thing his outfit included a flamboyantly-colored sweat band. But nothing could wipe the massive smile off his face. He looked like he was having the time of his life. I mean, he was the center of attention in front of a large crowd, so he probably was.

In fact, he *deffers* was.

There was a break in the music. The dancers were on their knees, nodding their heads, and Nick ran over to me, his sweet strawberry scent filling the air.

"Hey," he breathed heavily.

"Hey, yourself," I said, unable to contain a massive smile. "Fancy running into you like this."

He wrapped his arms around my neck.

"I have to go soon, my big dance number is coming up, but I just want to say two things real quick—I'm sorry, and I love you."

His sweet lips brushed against my cheek, and a moment later he was back in the middle of the makeshift dance floor, surrounded by all of the dancers.

And then...oh my God...Nick started breakdancing like a boss. He was a blur of knees, hands, jumps, and kicks. I had never seen anything like that. The moves he produced looked stunningly effortless. I knew they were anything but.

Man, that was one sexy boy.

I felt Stirling's hand on my shoulder.

"I told you you'd like this," he said with a smile.

We were all smiling. I'd been smiling so hard, I could feel wetness on my face. I brushed the tears of happiness away quickly and looked back at him.

My Nick.

My boy.

He was mine. Well, at least once this song was over and he had finished hurling all the dancers into the air in the big climactic finale. I tried to suppress the lawyer thoughts I was having about insuring something like this, and just watched and enjoyed it. Enjoyed him.

When it ended, the crowd that had gathered erupted into a loud roar of cheers and clapping. The dancers hugged each other and, slowly, the jubilation started to subside until all that could be heard was the sound of fingers furiously tapping at cell phone screens to upload what we had just witnessed onto social media.

Nick ran over to us, all sweaty, smiley, and happy.

"What did you think?" he asked. He was panting and out of breath. I wasn't surprised, that was quite the workout.

"I loved it," I said, drawing him in close and wrapping my arms around his saturated shirt. "And I love you."

"I love you so much, Steel," he said as his eyes began to well up.

"We should give you guys some privacy," Hudson said, tilting his head at Stirling and Porter in a sign they should leave.

"No, I think it's fine," Porter said, his eyes glued to us as if we were the movie that he was here to see. Somebody just needed to bring the man some popcorn and he would have been right at home. "I'm sure they don't mind us here."

"Actually," I said, hugging Nick protectively, "I might just bail on the movie and head home, if that's okay?"

"Of course," Stirling said as the others nodded. "We totally understand."

"Thanks," I said. "Will you be okay, Hudson? I know you were looking forward to it."

I couldn't resist teasing him. The gentle giant loved *Romy and Michele's High School Reunion*. I had a feeling we would be giving him crap about that for years to come.

"It's all good," he said with a knowing smile. "I've seen it like a million times. And the director's cut is much better than the cinema release anyway..." He only stopped when he saw four open mouths gaping at him in shock. "Uh, I was kidding?"

Stirling handed Nick a fluro-pink backpack. I had been wondering why he was wearing it. I had just put it down to Mikey's influence.

"Here's your stuff," he said to Nick.

"Thanks." Nick took the backpack.

We made our way to my car in silence.

"Where are we going? I thought we were going back to your place?" Nick asked when he realized I was taking a different route.

"We'll get to my place, but I want to show you something first."

"Okay."

A few minutes later, we pulled up in front of his grandparents' bakery. I studied his face as he looked at the building. The name of the bakery was still there, but the inside was completely empty. A big red 'SOLD' sign was splashed across the front window.

His head fell back into the seat.

"How are you feeling?" I asked. I needed to know what was going through his mind before I told him.

"You know what?" he said as he looked at me. "I'm actually okay. I think letting go of the bakery is actually a good thing for my grandparents."

"And what about you?"

"What about me?" His brown eyes were still peering out at the sold sign.

"Nick, it's clear this place means a lot to you. Are you ready to let it go?"

The words took up all of the space between us.

"Don't have much choice, do I?" he said as he looked at me. "It's already gone."

"Let's go home, huh?" I said, gently grazing his arm before driving away. Nick was quiet for the whole drive.

It hadn't taken me more than a few conversations with his grandparents when I had reached out to them after the accident to figure out how much Nick loved the bakery. In all honesty, he loved it way more than they did. Sure, it was the way they earned their living, but they were more than ready for something else. They wanted to travel and start a new chapter in their lives.

For Nick, though, the bakery was the grounding force in his life. It was filled with happy childhood memories. Ones that he wanted to hold on to. Ones that he would now be able to hold on to.

We still had a lot to talk about. As much as I knew in my heart of hearts that we were meant to be together, I didn't want to get ahead of myself either. It had hurt so much losing him once, I couldn't bear the thought of losing him again. I didn't think I would be able to survive that again.

No matter what happened tonight, or over the coming weeks, I was glad I'd done it. I'd stuck to the promise I'd made myself all those years ago. I had always sworn that I would turn the tragedy into a positive, into something good. And today, I had done just that.

I knew my parents would have been proud of me.

And for the record, I didn't do it to splash my money around, or to get back into Nick's good books.

No, I did it for one simple reason.

I loved him.

CHAPTER TWENTY-THREE

NICK

It was beyond unfair that flash mobs weren't eligible for Grammy awards, because what I had done tonight was some Grammy-level, award-winning stuff. From the choreography, to the dancers, to the detail in the outfits, we had succeeded in recreating the music video pretty much frame for frame.

The first sign that I should do it came to me while I was moping around my grandparents' house one lazy Wednesday afternoon. Well, every day had become a lazy day. I was feeling sorry for myself and consoling myself with a tub of Ben & Jerry's, scrolling mindlessly on my phone, watching everyone living lives that were so much better than mine.

I wasn't even paying attention to what was on the TV. So when the remote control fell behind my back without me realizing, and I squished it—also without realizing—and it turned to MTV, right at the start of the video for *Praise You*...yeah, I thought the big man upstairs was definitely giving a signal to this big boy downstairs.

It was a pretty darn catchy song and the video was way-out-there hilarious. I mean, in a totally '90s kind of way. The clothes alone were priceless and made me long for a time when fanny packs, wearing sweatpants in public, and retro-cool brown-striped shirts were back in fashion.

It managed to do something to me that I hadn't been able to do since I had stormed out of Steel's apartment the morning after I found out about his involvement in the deal. It made me smile.

It also made me get my big, lazy (and despite all of the shit I was going through, still amazingly bubbly and round) ass off the couch and into the basement, sorting through the mountains of miscellaneous boxes I had dumped in there.

I made three sorting piles—no, maybe, and deffers—and started going through the boxes, clearing them out one by one. Grandpa used the basement a lot so I wanted to clear some space for him to make sure that he never tripped or fell over my stuff. I wouldn't be able to deal with the guilt if that happened.

I was about five boxes in, which was barely making a dent, when I picked up a super cute, retro brown-striped shirt. I had completely forgotten I'd even picked it up on a thrift store shopping extravaganza with Mikey a few months before. Aside from it clinging to my round belly superbly, which I loved, it was also pretty much an exact replica of the lead dancer's shirt in the music video I had watched.

Hmm...was this another sign from God? Was I put on this earth to make '90s fashion cool again? I walked over to the mirror and placed the shirt across my chest, tilting my head and moving my body, imagining how fab-u-lous it would look on me.

That was when I got my third sign.

"Dinner's ready, Nick," Grandma's voice rang out from the top of the stairs.

That was when it hit me. I knew what to do.

As I made my way upstairs to dinner, it was another d-word that my grandmother had used that was ricocheting in my head.

There was nothing like being called a dick by your loving grandmother to really spur a boy into action.

Over the next two weeks, I dedicated myself to casting, choreographing, and rehearsing the best damn flash mob in human history. One that definitely deserved a Grammy. But in lieu of that, I was happy to take the look on Steel's face when he first saw me turn around and look at him out in front of the movie theater.

It was like a tsunami of happiness rushing out of him and spilling all over me. His eyes lit up and stayed lasered in on me for the entire routine. I felt so happy, so alive, so goddamn sexy dancing in front of him. I wanted him back more than ever.

I had been doing a lot of thinking and I realized it wasn't just Steel who had been a dick, it had been me as well. In fact, I might have even been the bigger dick. One time when that wasn't a good thing.

We needed to talk. I needed to apologize and to keep apologizing for as long as it took to make the man forgive me. How I hoped and prayed he would take me back.

I hadn't even realized we had pulled up in his basement parking lot until the engine cut off.

"Should I be worried?" Steel said, turning to me with his brow furrowed.

"What?" I asked absently.

"I don't think I've ever seen you this quiet, apart from when you've been sleeping."

He interlaced his fingers with mine and I met his warm smile with one of my own.

"We need to talk," I said.

He nodded his head and shifted slightly in his seat.

"We do. Let's go upstairs."

We were silent in the elevator.

We were silent as he grabbed two beers from the fridge.

We were silent until we finally sat down on his sofa and had each taken a swig of beer. I looked at the man sitting just a few feet away from me. This gorgeous man. His handsome face, his soft, tender lips that I loved kissing, his light blue eyes that would drill into my soul, the way his cock would drill into my ass.

I had been preparing for this moment almost as much as I had been rehearsing the dance routine. Now that it was here, though, my mind was blank and my throat felt tight. I took another big gulp of beer, the cold fizziness making its way down my throat, but not doing a whole lot to open it up.

I had a whole speech lined up, but now my mind was as blank as a fresh sheet of paper. A pain formed behind my eyes and I felt my hand shaking as I put the beer back down on the coffee table.

"I'm sorry, Steel," I managed to blurt out before the tears started rolling down my face. The more I brushed them away, the more they came.

Tears of embarrassment, because I had made such an idiot out of myself.

Tears of anger, because I had treated the man I loved so badly.

Tears of release, because I had been holding on to something that was no longer what my grandparents wanted.

I felt a gentle warmth envelop me and then Steel's steadying breath on my face as he held me, tight and close.

"I've got you baby," he said as he rocked me in his strong arms. He rubbed my back in long strokes, up and down, over and over again until he had soothed me.

I looked up at the man through tear-stained eyes.

"I had a whole speech planned, Steel. I wanted it to be funny and smart, and show you just how sorry I truly am. I shouldn't have left. I shouldn't have broken up with you."

Just saying those words released another flood of tears, followed by more soothing backrubs. How I had missed this man's touch.

"You've put on quite a show already tonight," he said as his lips lifted into a small smile. "And it was incredible."

"You liked it?" I said, batting my eyelids.

Hey, I didn't cry very often, but when I did, I knew I looked super adorable, so forgive me if I wanted to milk it for just one teensy-weensy second.

His smile unfolded like a blanket until it was covering his whole face.

"I loved it, baby," he said, dragging his fingers through my hair. "It was the single most amazing thing I've ever seen you do."

My body loosened a little.

"Better than when I was a naked butler?" I asked.

"Yep."

"Better than when you saw me go-go dancing at The Tank Top?"

"Yep."

"Better than the erotic cake-sitting scene I did at Revolver?"

"Yep."

Hmm...he was making this hard for me. I got it.

My eyes lit up as I asked, "Better than the time you fucked me against the windows?"

I tilted my head at the windows in question.

"Uh..." He looked unsure of himself, his smile crooked on his lips.

I leaned in and kissed him, grabbing the back of his neck and pulling his mouth closer to mine. I took him hungrily, urgently, as if I hadn't eaten in a week.

He kissed back, just as hard. Harder. Pulling me in and running his hands across my chest, pinching my nipples underneath my brown-striped shirt. I groaned into his mouth and the vibration that it caused almost made me come in my pants right there and then.

"Hang on," he said, pulling away from me. The light blue of his eyes contrasted so beautifully with the bright pink of his swollen, just-been-kissed lips. "Before neither one of us can think straight, I need to show you something."

"Is it your massive cock?" I asked, looking up at him as he got off the sofa and stood up.

"No," he said with a smirk, but the tentpole in his jeans was saying *yes*. "Wait right here. I'll be back in a minute."

My eyes dragged up and down his body as he left the room.

When he returned a few moments later, he had a bunch of blue and manilla folders in his hands.

"Did you print out all of your dick pics so that I would have physical copies?" I asked hopefully.

He laughed. "Not exactly. I need to show you a couple of non-dick-related things."

He sat down next to me on the couch and handed me a blue folder.

"I want to explain my trust fund to you," he said. I opened my mouth to say something but he raised a hand in the air. "Please let me."

I bit down on my lip and nodded.

"You were right about the trust fund. I did inherit money when I turned twenty-one. My parents died in a car crash a few weeks after I turned nineteen."

"Oh my God, Steel, I'm so sorry. I didn't know that."

Damn, I hadn't read the whole article, so I must have missed that bit. A fucking horrific, awful detail to miss. A pang of hurt filled my chest. His eyes grew a little misty, but he continued.

"I did come from money. Old money on my father's side. But my parents wanted to raise me as normally as they could."

I nodded, listening carefully to every word he was saying, determined not to miss another detail ever again.

"Don't get me wrong, I still had privilege dripping out of my ass," he said, and we both chuckled. "I had the best of everything and I never wanted for anything. But my parents did a good job with me. I wasn't spoiled or entitled. I was raised with a healthy respect for the very good fortune our family enjoyed."

I studied his face. I could see his jaw tensing, but when he spoke, the lines around his eyes softened, as if they were searching for the good memories that were hidden amongst the bad.

"Losing my parents was the worst thing that ever happened to me," he continued, his voice surprisingly strong and firm. "But I never wanted to remember them for how they died. I wanted to remember them for how they lived. It was my way of honoring them."

He took another mouthful of beer, and paused for a moment to look at me before he continued.

"They left me that trust fund, not so that I would use it, or blow it, but as insurance. It was to be used as a backup if my life went to shit, because I wouldn't have them to support me through anything. So that's how I approached it."

We both looked down at the blue folder in my lap.

"What I just gave you is a copy of my bank statement. Well, actually, the bank statement of my trust fund."

"Oh," I said, looking down at the unopened folder. I felt an uneasiness rising within me, but I didn't say anything.

"Open it," Steel said, and so I did.

I didn't know what I was looking at. I wasn't exactly the corporate type. Until I had been corrected a few months ago, I thought an Excel spreadsheet was the name of a dance move. I guessed that's what I was looking at here, rows and rows and rows of numbers that made literally no sense to me at all.

"Look up at the top right-hand corner," Steel said, reading the confusion on my face. "What number do you see?"

"Uh..." I squinted to see. My eyes bulged. "Holy shit. Ten million dollars."

"Right," Steel said with a firm nod. "That's how much money my trust fund had when the account was opened twenty years ago. Now if you turn over to the very last page..."

I had never seen Steel in lawyer mode before, and damn, if it wasn't doing things to me that made me think we should bring this up in future role-playing. I followed his instruction and turned to the last page of the thick document.

"Now look down to the bottom of the page," Steel directed me. "What number do you see in the bottom row?"

I looked down. "Forty million dollars," I replied.

"Right, that's the power of compound interest for you. It just grew and grew each year."

It took my brain a few seconds to process the meaning behind Steel's words.

"Wait, so you're saying that you've never used any of this money?" I was in total disbelief.

"That's right," he said as he looked me in the eyes. It felt like he was staring straight into my soul and I was staring straight back into his. "I made a promise to myself that I would never touch that money until I turned at least forty. And then if I did use it for anything, it would be for something good."

"So you really are a self-made man, then?" I said softly, and I wanted to punch myself over and over again for misjudging him so badly.

"Yeah, I guess I am," he replied, falling back onto the sofa. "I'm a hard worker, I'm passionate, and I'm disciplined. I got a good start in life for sure, but the rest I did on my own."

"Wow."

What the hell else was there to say? Everything I had thought about Steel, everything that I'd held against him—that he wasn't really self-made like everyone thought, that he was a rich, spoiled trust fund baby—all of it had just been blown up in my face.

Suddenly I felt like the biggest jerk in the world. I steadied my breathing, not wanting to cry. This wasn't about me, this was about the most amazing man I had ever met.

"I'm so sorry I misjudged you so badly." The words felt heavy coming out of my mouth, but they were the right words. The exact words that I wanted to say right there and then to him. I'd never meant an apology more.

"Thank you, Nick," he said, letting out a deep breath and placing his hands on his knees. "That means a lot to me."

We looked at each other only briefly, but the love that we felt was as visible as fireflies sparkling against a pitch-black sky, flying between us, around us, and filling the entire apartment.

"I should have told you sooner, but I liked the fact that you were one of the few people that I knew who didn't like me for my money. You have no idea how refreshing and rare that is."

That part was true. I didn't care about his money, never had. I enjoyed being independent and being able to look after myself. It meant a lot to me to be able to do that. I just wished I hadn't fucked everything up so badly.

He shuffled across the sofa. He stared deep into my eyes as he brushed a few loose strands of hair behind my ear. Our lips and the tips of our noses pressed softly against each other, sending tingles of pleasure all the way down to my feet. We didn't move for what felt like an eternity.

It was the sweetest kiss I had ever had in my whole life.

When he pulled away, the coldness felt like an Arctic breeze hitting me.

"Come back, I liked that," I said.

He smiled and tilted his head, his eyes flitting across my face.

"I've got one more thing to show you." As I opened my mouth to say what we both knew I was going to say, he beat me to it. "One more non-dick-related thing, that is."

"Fine," I said, crossing my arms and pretending to be more upset than I really was.

He picked up a manilla folder from the table and handed it to me.

"What is this?" I asked as I opened it.

"It's the trust fund's latest bank statement. From today. See the number there?" He tapped on the paper and I nodded. It wasn't forty million dollars anymore. It was less. I mean, still impressive, but less.

"I don't understand." I looked up at him and for the first time that evening, he looked content and calm.

"Turn the page," he said with a wink.

I did. The words *Deed of Sale* were written across the top in a bold font. My eyes scanned further down until my heart flew out of my mouth, smack-bang onto the couch.

I looked up at him, hot tears spilling out of my eyes.

"You bought the bakery?" I said, my whole body trembling.

"No," Steel said with a smile. "I bought the whole damn building, including the bakery."

I couldn't believe what this man had done.

"I think you will do an amazing job running the bakery. *Your* bakery."

"My—my bakery?" I stammered.

He nodded, his eyes were lit up and the excitement was pouring out of him.

"And my friends and I, we need a good damn bar to hang out in," he added with a laugh.

CHAPTER TWENTY-FOUR

STEEL

Nick's tears melted me.

I was definitely hoping for a reaction—the boy was incredibly expressive after all—but I had been envisioning laughter and smiles and jumping up and down. Lots of jumping up and down.

Not tears. Even though I knew they were happy tears, they still tugged at my heart.

"Why did you do all of this?" he asked, wiping at his eyes.

A fullness settled in my chest.

"Because I wanted to do something good," I finally said, taking my time to find the exact right words. "Don't get me wrong, the developers had really good plans for the place. But they would change the area quite dramatically, and for some reason, I didn't want that to happen. I wanted something of the old to remain while making the place new and exciting."

I looked over at Nick who was just listening to me, blinking his gorgeous big brown eyes at me, but just listening.

"I'm rambling, aren't I?" I said with a low chuckle.

He shook his head.

"No, I get it. I feel the same way about the bakery. I get that my grandparents wanted to leave it behind and enjoy the rest of their lives, but a part of me wanted to keep it, you know?"

"Well, now you can," I said as I leaned in to steal a kiss. Nick's lips brushed against mine as I closed my eyes, enjoying this sweet moment. I had Nick back in my apartment, back in my life again. But then he suddenly, sharply, pulled away from me.

"You did all of this before my Grammy-award-winning performance tonight," he said seriously. Well, as seriously as someone could say something like that.

"Grammy-award-winning?" I raised my eyebrows and cocked my head to the side.

He smiled just a little and gave a shrug. The cutest shrug ever.

"I did," I said, clearing my throat. "I didn't know what was happening with us, and to be clear, I didn't do this so that we would get back together."

"You don't want to get back together?" Nick asked, chewing on his lower lip.

"I do. I very much do," I began. "But I just wanted to make it clear that this wasn't some attempt to buy you back into my life."

It really wasn't.

Yes, I wanted him to keep the bakery, but I also wanted the other businesses in the building—the hair and nail salon, the dry cleaner, the day spa, the small grocery store, and the empty dive bar —to stay.

Especially the dive bar. I had big plans for that place.

He looked like he was seriously considering what I was saying, mulling it over in his head as his eyes shifted around the room.

"I mean, it is one helluva grand gesture," he said, before adding with a wicked, wide smile. "It's kinda like what you see in the movies."

"So what happens in the movie after the guy does the grand gesture?" I asked, smiling back at him.

"Well, in the movies that I like, he wins the guy back and they go on to live happily ever after...after they have mindblowingly amazing sex, that is."

"Hmm," I said bringing my thumb and index finger to my chin. "I like the movies you watch, Nick Macklin."

"God, you're hot." It was all I heard.

The next thing I knew, Nick was straddling my chest and peppering my face with greedy, hungry, sloppy, wet kisses. His strawberry scent was heavy on his breath.

How I'd missed his smell.

His taste.

The fullness of his body pressed into mine.

I ran my fingers through his long brown hair, messing it up a little as I tickled his scalp with my fingertips. He moaned at the touch and I invaded his mouth, reclaiming what was mine and making up for lost time. All that lost time.

I should have been honest with Nick sooner and not kept things from him. If I had done that, I could have avoided a whole bunch of heartache for both of us.

"I'm so sorry, Steel," he panted in between kisses. "I shouldn't have judged you the way I did. I should have talked to you."

"Hey," I said, cupping his face with my hands to steady him for a moment. "The lesson here is—we *both* should have talked more." I smiled and Nick did too, but for just the tiniest moment, something else flashed through his eyes.

He flinched, but said nothing other than, "I deffers agree."

"I've missed you so much, Nick."

"I've missed you so much too, Steel. Now get your cock inside of me."

"Wow, do they say that in your movies too?" We both laughed.

I grabbed both of Nick's hands, and with all of my strength, pulled myself up off the couch and flipped him around, so that now, I was the one on top of him.

"Mmm...I like this," he said, and the words sounded deliciously sweet and utterly filthy at same time.

I felt his hands fumbling with my belt buckle. My boy was desperate to get my pants off, and his hands—and mouth—on my cock. I had absolutely no objection to that at all.

He managed to pull my pants down and my cock practically hit him in the face as it flew out of my briefs.

"Careful there, *Daddy*..." Fuck, if hearing him say that word didn't make me almost black out with sheer happiness. "You could take an eye out with that thing."

He smiled and licked his lips at the same time.

He wrapped his fingers around the base of my cock, sliding his fist up and down with a firm pressure.

"It's a little dry, Daddy. You might need to stick it in my mouth so I can get it nice and wet for you." Okay, we were definitely not in a PG-rated movie anymore, things were getting very X-rated...and fast. "Can you pass me a pillow?"

I reached around and grabbed a couch pillow from behind me. He lifted his head and I gently placed it underneath him to give him the support he needed. He was now perfectly positioned. The head of my cock was less than a tantalizing inch away from his very open and very willing mouth.

He looked up at me as he took the swollen head of my dick between his sweet pink lips. He kept his intense, heavy gaze focused on me as he swallowed me down until my entire length disappeared into his mouth.

He pulled about halfway out and then slammed back all the way down again. And again. And again. My boy wanted his Daddy to throat fuck him. And if that was what my boy wanted, that was exactly what my boy would get.

I placed my hands on the sides of his face, holding him in place. He moaned in anticipation and the vibration tore through my entire body. Keeping him perfectly still with both of my hands, I began to rock forward and backward, only putting half the length of my cock inside of his mouth before sliding it back out again.

Gradually I increased the depth, making sure to give him enough time to adjust to my size. I saw his jaw unclench and I knew that it was time to give him what he wanted. All of me.

"Are you ready?" I asked as I pulled out of him. I wanted a clear *yes* first.

"Yes...Daddy. I want you so badly. Please."

I smiled. Good. I slowly pushed my cock until it was fully in his mouth. Then I asked again.

"You sure you're ready for Daddy?" I had gotten my clear *yes*, now I wanted my mouth-stuffed-full-of-cock *yes*.

"Yempfh."

The vibration from the back of his throat hummed throughout my entire body. Not waiting a single second longer, I gave my boy what he wanted. Long, deep, firm strokes of cock filled his mouth. His lips slurped and swallowed my cock until I thought I would blow.

I wasn't ready to do that yet. Oh no, the night had only just begun.

I pulled out of his mouth one last time, and looked down at my cock glistening with my boy's saliva, and his beautiful lips, all puckered and pink and swollen.

"What are you doing?" His voice was low and coarse.

"I'm doing what they do at the end of movies," I said. "I'm going to carry you into my bedroom and fuck you until you can't come anymore."

"Uh..." A serious look fell over Nick's face.

"What is it, baby?" I asked, tidying up the hair I'd spent the last half hour messing up.

"Well," he started. "In the movies, the main characters are usually a size nothing. I'm a size everything."

"And I love every single part of you, Nick," I said, tracing my fingers along the smattering of light hairs that covered his solid chest.

"You're not going to break my ass this time?"

"Stop saying that," I said with a gentle pinch on his nipple which he immediately twisted his body into. "You sprained your tailbone...*mildly*."

"Well stop saying *tailbone*," he said, sticking his tongue out playfully.

"You don't like that word?"

"No, it makes me sound like I'm some animal. Some animal with a tail." We both laughed.

"Well you are an animal," I said, peeling myself off him. "Especially in the bedroom."

I reached my hand out and helped him up off the sofa.

"I won't break you," I said with a soft kiss.

"You promise?" he asked, his brown eyes filled with a vulnerability that I would treasure and protect at all costs.

I picked him up and held him across my chest, his legs dangling over the side of my body.

"Deffers," I said as I carried him into my bedroom.

"Hey, don't steal my catchphrase," he said with a sweet laugh that rocked his entire body.

I had him firmly in my grip, holding onto him like he was the most valuable thing in the world.

Because he was.

As soon as I placed him gently down on my bed, the heat between us turned back up to scorching. Our mouths smashed into each other as he grabbed my cock and began to furiously jack me off.

"I want you inside of me," he said in between our hungry, messy kisses. His warm breath filled my mouth, and I wanted nothing more than to fill him up too. Being inside of my boy was the best feeling in the world.

I grabbed the lube and condoms from my bedside table. I

slicked two fingers up and pressed them firmly against his hole, feeling the twitchy entrance inviting me in.

He let out an ecstatic moan as I drew the fingers deeper into him, his warmth encasing them. His body was already on fire and I hadn't even begun. I played with him for just a few more moments, sliding my fingers in and out of his ass, enjoying the sight of his body quivering at my touch.

"I'm ready, I'm ready, I'm ready," he panted.

"Oh, is that so?" I said as I slid the condom right down to the base of my granite-hard cock.

"Don't tease me, Steel...I can't bear it. Please. *Please.*"

My cock ached so hard at the sound of his needy pleas that it actually hurt. In the best possible way. I greased up my dick and slid it inside of my boy. His body bucked wildly underneath me, but there was no resistance. No, if anything there was encouragement. For more. My boy wanted more.

And that was exactly what he got. We started off fucking in the bed, before moving to the white marble kitchen countertop. Then we decided to get some fresh air...so we fucked on the rooftop, then in front of the floor-to-ceiling windows, then back in the kitchen, and then finally back on the bed where it had all started.

"I've got something to show you," Nick said, and as he lay himself down on the bed, he threw his legs up into the air and then down over his head, exposing his beautiful round ass and gaping hole to me. He knew how much I loved the sight of his body, but I had never seen him like this.

"Are you okay?"

While I definitely appreciated the view, I didn't know if being contorted like a pretzel would be comfortable for him.

"Hey, big boys can be flexible too," he said. "But I'd be a lot more comfortable if you were fucking me."

"Uh...okay...and how would I do that exactly?" I asked. Whatever movie he had gotten this crazy position from had suddenly made it to the top of my must-watch list.

"Rest your feet on the headboard, plank out your body, line your dick up with my hole and then start doing push-ups. Let's put those muscles of yours to good use."

He never failed to surprise me, but I didn't hesitate to follow his tricky instructions, and when I did...holy shit, it was the best feeling in the world. Yes, it felt a bit like a workout because I was technically doing push-ups, but with each downward thrust, I plunged deeper into my boy.

It was obviously filling him at just the right angle, because before we both knew it, his ass clenched and he started to come. His release spilled out onto his neck and covered his whole chest.

That did it and my orgasm finally reached me as well, tearing through my entire body. The muscles in my arms twitched and I had to get off them and be beside my boy immediately. I swivelled around until I was lying next to him.

I reached for him and pulled him in close. I could see his pearly white release glistening on his flushed skin and I swooped down to clean it up with my tongue. The salty-sweet taste filled my mouth, and I lapped at it all until there was nothing left.

When I was done, our bodies wrapped into each other. I cradled him in my arms as we rocked ever so gently, both coming down from the euphoric high of what had been the most unforgettable night of my entire life.

CHAPTER TWENTY-FIVE

NICK

The warmth of Steel's breath felt like butter on warm toast against the back of my neck as my body cooled down from the best sex I had ever had. Although, I should probably stop saying that. Every time I had sex with Steel felt like the best sex of my life.

But yeah, that crazy legs-over-my-head position was something else...deffers. And judging by how Steel's body was shaking violently both while and after he came, it made me think he liked it too. A lot.

I was so happy to be back in his arms, and back with my Daddy. It's funny how there were so many things we didn't talk about.

Like me calling him *Daddy*.

Maybe Steel had thought that I wasn't *that kind of boy* because in so many other areas, I *wasn't*. I wasn't the typical boy in that I wasn't shy or quiet or reserved. Not that all boys were those things, but I literally had none of that in me. Not even the tiniest bit.

But he never talked about what he wanted to be called. And I never brought it up either. I didn't know if it was something he even wanted. So neither one of us ever knew where we stood on me calling him *Daddy*. I had slipped out a few *Da-dudes* when I lived with him, but that was about as far as it had gone.

I didn't mind calling him *Daddy*. In fact, I really liked it...a lot. It's just that it wasn't something I wanted to do as much as, say, Mikey did with Stirling. For me, it was really only a bedroom thing and maybe occasionally a private thing, when it was just the two of us alone at home. I couldn't imagine doing it out in public or in front of other people.

It was a conversation we needed to have.

I also felt bad, really bad actually, that I had never brought up all of the stuff about Steel's trust fund before either. If I had, it would have cleared things up and I would have seen him for the amazing man that I knew he was. Instead, I caused both of us so much pain. I was so, so sorry I had done that, and I knew deep inside that I would do everything I could to never hurt Steel like that again.

I still couldn't believe what he had done for me. Not only was it a super-duper romantic gesture, but it showed me something else. It showed me that he knew me, like, really knew me, maybe even better than I knew myself. I mean, I really thought my grandparents were attached to the bakery, but maybe I was more attached to it than they were?

Another thing we would have to figure out was the money side of Steel's grand gesture. I was not some money-hungry boy looking for a sugar daddy. I was an independent, hard-working boy, and however things worked out, I would repay Steel for buying the bakery, one way or another.

Part of me was so excited about it. As much as I loved my eclectic jobs, something felt really good about dedicating myself to just one thing. I loved that bakery with all of my heart. It had so many good memories for me and I couldn't wait to see what I could do with the place. I wanted to turn it around and make it profitable so badly, and now I had that chance. I might even get to use a spreadsheet one day, ooh how business-y of me!

It wasn't easy for me to accept help at the best of times, but I knew I had to work through that. Steel hadn't bought the bakery to buy me or buy my love. He wasn't the type of man who would lord this over me.

No, he'd done it because he wanted to. There were no secret strings attached. Which was how I needed to accept it. Honestly, with humility and with a ton of hard work, to show him that his decision really was the right one. It was his trust fund, after all, something he hadn't touched for over twenty years. That was serious, and that was how I would approach the bakery.

And while we were on the topic of things we needed to talk about, there was one more thing I needed to add to the list.

I chewed on my lip, trying to figure out if this was the right moment or if I should wait. No, waiting would be a cop-out. I would keep finding reasons to put it off and never get around to it...again. I had to learn my lesson of the past few weeks and that meant talking to Steel about something I had never spoken to anyone about.

I rolled over to look at him. My man. My Daddy. His silver hair was all messy and his light blue eyes were lit up like the sun reflecting on the ocean. He was staring dreamily at me, his fingers lazily grazing my jaw.

"Can—can we talk?" I asked.

Wrinkles covered his forehead as he sat up a little straighter in the bed.

"Of course, baby." His voice was the soothing tonic I needed. "What is it?"

I looked away from him until I felt his fingers gently tilting my face up. His eyes were so warm and filled with genuine affection.

"You can talk to me about anything, baby," he said. "I know talking hasn't been our strong suit so far, but let's change that, okay?"

I swallowed hard.

"Okay, I have to tell you something," I said.

He lifted my hand and placed it into his, gently stroking the back of it with his thumb. His touch calmed me.

"I think I might be into something..."

"Uh huh," he said, nodding his head ever so slightly.

"Something...sexual..."

He smiled, bringing my hand up to his lips and giving it a kiss.

"Is it as crazy hot as whatever that position was you got into before?" he asked, and we both smiled at each other, but the smile quickly vanished from my face.

"I—I don't know," I stammered. There was so much I still didn't know about what I liked, or what I thought I liked, or what I thought I could maybe possibly like one day. But I did know one thing for sure.

I wanted to tell Steel, and I wanted us to figure it out together, as boy and Daddy.

My heart was thumping so hard in my chest I thought it would break out.

"Do you remember how I got upset with you when I overheard you calling someone a big, fat, stupid baby on the yacht at Hudson's fortieth?" I asked.

I could see the look of embarrassment flood his face and tighten his jaw.

"I do," he said, his voice laced with regret.

I cleared my throat. "Well, it wasn't just the fact that you were calling someone big and fat that really hurt me. It was that you called them a baby."

His expression went from embarrassment to confusion as he stared straight into me. I took a deep breath, grimaced and then just came right out and said it.

"I think I might be into age play." I closed my eyes and sank into the darkness and the silence that followed my words.

Oh no, what was he thinking? That I was an idiot? A freak?

Not worth being with? Damn...I'd ruined it. I mentally cursed myself. Just as we finally got our shit together, I had to go ahead and ruin it. I couldn't believe what I had done. The panic raised my heartrate through the roof.

I peeked one eye open.

Steel was looking at me. His face was neutral and annoyingly unreadable. I didn't know what to think. He hadn't bolted and he hadn't kicked me out, so that was good, right? But he also wasn't saying anything either. That was less good.

"Let me show you something," he said, getting up off the bed. My eyes followed him but I didn't move. "Come on," he said as he opened the top drawer of the bedside table, grabbed something out of it, and then motioned for me to follow him out the door.

I did and we padded barefoot and naked out of his room, across the lounge, and down the hallway.

"What are we doing?" I asked as we reached the end of the hallway and the mystery room that I had never been inside.

"This," he said as he raised his hand to reveal a shiny gold key. He opened the bedroom door with it and reached for my hand. He flicked the light switch on as we entered the bedroom although it looked more like a...nursery.

Holy shitballs.

I gasped as my breath caught in my throat, taking it all in. It was so beautiful. The walls were each painted a different bright and bold color—one green, one blue, and one yellow. There were a number of see-through crates filled with all sorts of fun-looking toys, and smack-bang in the middle of the room was a large, clearly adult-sized wooden crib.

I had only ever seen rooms like this online, but standing in one right now did something to my insides. I felt so at ease and even though I was only seeing it for the first time in my life, it felt like I was...coming home. There was something so familiar about it, like all of my thoughts and hopes and desires had become real. Because they had.

"What—what is all of this?" I asked when I was finally able to speak. I looked over at Steel.

He was looking around the room himself and there was a gleam in his eye that I didn't recognize.

"Something I've been wanting to explore, I guess," he said, turning to look at me. "I haven't done anything with anyone here," he quickly added. "I've been waiting for the right boy."

"Why didn't you tell me you were into this?" I asked as I took a step forward.

"Why didn't *you?*" he asked as he took my hand in his. "I assumed—incorrectly, I now see—that you weren't interested in this, and I didn't want to do anything to jeopardize our relationship."

The list of things we had not talked about grew longer by the minute. As I looked around the room, I made a promise to myself in that moment that I would never, ever keep anything from this man again. No matter how hard, or weird, or uncomfortable it was, I would talk to him and tell him whatever it was that was going on for me.

I nodded. I could completely relate to what he was saying. That was what had kept me from talking too. Whether it was about what I had overheard him saying on the yacht, or what I had assumed about his trust fund situation, I thought that by raising something tough or prickly, it would destroy what we had.

What I was quickly learning was that *not* talking was the only thing that could potentially destroy us.

"Besides, like you, I'm brand new to all of this. Apart from watching some scenes at Revolver, and talking to some Daddies there about it, I haven't had any personal experience with it."

"You haven't?" I asked softly.

He shook his head. "No." His voice was firm. "I knew this was something I liked and wanted to explore. But I guess—I guess I hadn't found the right boy to do that with. But I wanted to be ready when I did."

His words made my heart flutter. It was like we had both been waiting for each other to try this...together. I shivered with happiness and also because I was starting to get cold.

"Let's go back to bed," Steel said, noticing how my body was shaking. "It's warmer in there."

I nodded and we made our way back to the bedroom in silence. As I got into the bed, he lifted up the comforter for me. When I was ready, he placed it over me, tucking me in nice and tight, making sure it was wrapped well around my entire body. It felt so good, so safe. Like I was being looked after by my Daddy.

He got in the bed beside me, resting on his elbow. His face, his eyes, his whole body was glowing. Just our feet were touching but it was enough to send a fierce heat through my entire body.

"How are you feeling?" he asked as he brushed a loose strand of hair off my face.

"Good," I replied. "A little surprised, but in a good way."

A very good way. Could Steel and I actually make this work? I mean, I was unconventional, to say the least. Could we be boyfriends in life, a Daddy and his boy in the bedroom, and then also a Daddy and his...little?

Could a big boy like me really be a little?

Would I be a good little?

Would I even like it?

Would Steel?

What if one of us liked it and the other one didn't?

What if...?

"Let's just relax and take our time with this," Steel said, finding just the words I needed to hear to stop my mind from splintering into a million different what-ifs. "With all of it. You and me, the bakery, the...other things we'd like to explore. There's no rush with any of it, okay, Nick?"

I looked up into my Daddy's handsome face and nodded. He truly was the man of my dreams. Perfect in every way.

"Are you sure you want to be with me?" I asked him, giving him the last chance I would ever give the man to get out and take that escape clause. If he wasn't sure, if he had even the slightest doubt, this was it. His very last chance to get out.

"Oh, I'm sure, baby," he said.

"Really and truly?"

A smile lit up his whole face.

"Deffers," he said. And with that, he leaned into me and gave me a soft kiss that turned into a long, deep, passionate kiss.

Cue the camera as it starts off in an extreme close-up of both of our faces, our tongues twirling around in each other's mouths, our hands all over our faces. Then it pulls away and the last thing anyone sees is the sight of one over-the-moon big boy, wrapped up in the arms of his loving, amazing Daddy.

Then the screen fades to black.

EPILOGUE

NICK

The door to the limousine was opened for me, and before I could even set foot on the shimmering red carpet, the sound of cameras flashing and people screaming my name filled the air.

"Nick! Nick!"

There were lights and the sound of screaming all around me, and for a minute, it felt just a little overwhelming. But that minute passed by real quick as I dazzled the world with my smile, ready to make my stunning red carpet debut at the Academy Awards.

Never in my wildest dreams could I have imagined that *Big: The Movie* would do so well. It totally killed it at the box office and it spurred a whole line of *deffers* merchandising—stickers, lunchboxes, shirts (plus-size friendly, of course)—you name it, and there was a good chance *deffers* was plastered all over it. Things blew up so much and everything me-related became so popular that there was even a strawberry bubblegum shortage by the end of summer. Yeah, that's how big it got.

"Can I take your hand?" Chris Hemsworth asked in that rich Australian accent of his. He stepped out of the car after me. But he wasn't my date.

"No, let *me* take his hand."

I turned around to see a stern-looking Chris Evans giving Chris Hemsworth the death stare.

"Guys, it's my turn. I still haven't had the chance to hold his hand on a red carpet yet."

I think that was Chris Pine, he's around here somewhere too.

"Guys, we all agreed," Chris Pratt said as he stepped through the sea of Chrises around me and grabbed me by my hand. "I did the cake-sitting scene, I walk him down the red carpet at the Oscars. That was the deal, remember?"

And with that, Chris Pratt and I walked down the red carpet, hand-in-hand, with the other three Chrises—all looking mighty fine in their tuxedos, let me tell you—walking behind us trying to mask their disappointment. They're actors, it shouldn't be that hard.

Casting turned out to be quite the challenge. No one Chris captured all of me, so the casting director decided to make a very bold choice. They went with all four Chrises to play me at various stages of my life. It was a good decision and the critics ate it up. We were coming off some big wins at all the other award ceremonies, but everyone knew it all came down to this night.

I was positively glowing and looking every bit the Hollywood star in my green velvet three-piece tuxedo. It made my shoulders look broad, accentuated the thickness through my middle nicely, and gave me ass for days. I would be making a lot of hot lists with this look.

I could deffers get used to this. A dreamboat Chris on my arm, cameras flashing all around me, people screaming at me, yelling out all sorts of lovely things at me.

"*Nick, we love you!*"

"*Nick, who are you wearing? You look amazing!*"

"Nick, wake the fuck up," Mikey said, tugging at my forearm as he leaned over the counter.

"Oh, hey, Mikey," I said, straightening up. "When did you get here?"

"Like, five minutes ago. I was enjoying watching you totally space out, but then you started drooling."

"Oh shit, did I?" I looked down at the glass countertop I had been leaning against. "You liar."

Mikey erupted in laughter.

"Made you look though," he said as he took off his jacket.

"What are you doing here?" I asked. It was mid-morning and Mikey had classes most days.

"Stirling came by to check on the progress happening next door, so I thought I'd tag along too. I don't have classes until this afternoon."

I nodded. "Can I get you anything?"

When I'd taken over the bakery, I had added a whole bunch of new tasty treats to the menu. Mikey, with his natural auburn and Nick-approved hair color, eyed the display cabinet, chewing on his lip.

"Ooh, what are those things?" he asked, pointing at the second row of treats.

"They're chocolate eclairs. Pastry, cream, and chocolate heaven. You've never had one?" Mikey shook his head. "Well, you are going to love it."

I gave Mikey the eclair and the look of ecstasy that spread across his face made my heart warm.

"Holy shit, this is amazing," he said after taking a bite.

"It is, Mikey boy," I said with a grin. "And now I know what your sex face looks like too."

"Believe me," Mikey said as he looked me straight in the eye. "This doesn't even come close to my sex face."

Mikey was getting more and more confident every time I saw him, and I couldn't be happier.

"Should we go next door and see how things are going?" he asked.

"Yep," I said. "Let me just grab my jacket from out back."

Mikey followed me into the back office. There wasn't much to it: a desk, a couple of chairs, and a computer that I had finally figured out how to turn on after six months. That was about it. Oh, and a picture of my grandparents hanging on the wall.

Mikey walked over to the gold-framed photo and sighed wistfully as he traced his fingers along it. "It's so sad they're not here to see you running this place," he said as I walked up next to him.

"I know," I said, looking at the photo as I put my jacket on.

"Do you miss them?" He turned to look at me, sadness filling his big blue eyes.

"I do," I said, zipping up my jacket. "But they're having the best time ever in Paris. I talk to them every day and they're the ones sending me awesome ideas for bakery treats. This week, it's chocolate eclairs, next week it's chocolate croissants."

"Ooh, how fancy," Mikey said with a laugh. "I'm happy they're happy."

"Me too," I said. "Now let's go next door and see what those Daddies of ours are getting up to. They've been banging away all morning, scaring all my customers away."

It was true, they had been, but I didn't mind a little bit of noise. I was happy, well and truly happy. I had my bakery, my grandparents were travelling the world and living out their dream, my best friend was by my side, and best of all, I had my Daddy.

I put the *Back in 10* sign on the door and grabbed Mikey around the waist as we headed to the bar right next to the bakery.

STEEL

.   .   .

"Guys, take a beat. Go grab a coffee and come back in twenty minutes," I yelled out, and the drilling, scraping, screeching sounds all came to a halt. Although, I was pretty sure I could still hear a ringing in my ears. The crew of six workers laid down their tools and made their way outside.

We'd been making a lot of noise since early in the morning. But doing up a dive bar and turning it into something Laird-level was going to take some hard work. If that meant a little noise, then so be it. It would be worth it if for no other reason than me and my friends finally having a bar we enjoyed hanging out at.

"So tell me again how all of this works," Porter said, looking around at what looked like more of a construction site than the interior of Daylesford's next hot Daddy bar.

The guys had come down for a mid-morning inspection to check on the progress we were making. Construction had only started a month ago and the vision was still a while away from being realized.

I talked them through the main design points. The bar was staying where it was, but was being totally ripped up. The old faded brown panels were gone and in their place there would be a shimmering jewel of glass in the center of the bar. Comfortable leather and velvet booths would line the walls and there would be space for a stage, band, and dance floor.

"Yeah, I think TV and the internet have ruined my imagination," Hudson said with a chuckle when I had finished talking. "I can't see it."

"Me either," Porter said. "But I'm sure it'll be great, Steel. Although, how are you going to run a law firm and a bar at the same time? And you're also a Daddy now, don't forget."

"I wouldn't want to forget that," I said with a grin.

"And you've got a lot on your hands with that boy," Porter added with a cheeky smile. "Figuratively and literally."

Didn't I know it. The last six months had been the happiest time of my life. Nick had moved back in with me, he was doing great things turning the bakery around. It was close to becoming profitable again and we were in a really good place.

He was learning to trust me more and to let me help him, without feeling like he was weak or a burden to me. That was a lot for him to deal with and he was processing it slowly, taking lots of small steps in the right direction.

I was finding my feet in the relationship too. Being a Daddy to a bratty boy is a whole world unto itself. I always wanted it, and I loved it, though I did feel like I was out of my depth sometimes.

But no matter what was happening with either one of us, the biggest lesson that we had learned was a simple one. Talking. No matter how hard it was or how much we didn't want to do it, we always checked in with each other and made sure we talked about what was going on between us.

That really was the foundation for any good relationship, and lately, we'd been talking about something very interesting indeed. Age play. Maybe the time was right. Maybe it was something that we could look at introducing into our relationship. But we still needed to figure some stuff out and keep talking while we did.

"So tell me about the name of this place," Porter said, looking in my direction.

"What do you want to know about it?" I asked, feigning ignorance. I looked over at Hudson and Stirling, they were both smiling.

"It's a little...out there," Porter said. He looked like he was choosing his words carefully, which was very uncharacteristic for the guy who had literally zero tact. "I mean...*Deffers?*"

"It's a good name," I said with a shrug. "And it was my idea."

"It was?" Stirling asked.

I nodded. "Yes, I got it from Nick, but I like it. I think it's catchy and it's unique and it has a good ring to it."

"My ears are burning," Nick's voice rang out as we all turned to look at him and Mikey walking through the construction zone toward us.

"Hey, baby," I said as he cuddled into me, as Mikey snuggled into Stirling.

"Hey, Daddy," he whispered softly, so that only I could hear. We had agreed to only use that term at home or when it was just the two of us, but if he wanted to use it at any other time, that was fine with me. More than fine actually, I loved it.

"We were just talking about the name of the bar," Porter said, filling the boys in.

"It's amazing, isn't it?" Nick said, flashing a wide toothy smile. I loved seeing my boy so proud and preening.

"Deffers?" Porter said, not sounding entirely convinced...yet. He'd come around.

"So the next big question is..." I said as I looked around the room. "Who will be the next Daddy to get a boy, Porter or Hudson?"

"Smart money's on Hudson," Porter said with a grin. "I am nowhere near ready to settle down yet. I haven't sowed my oats enough."

"Uh, I think you've sowed your oats over every boy in Daylesford," Stirling joked.

Laughter erupted and he cuddled into Mikey even more. It was good seeing him joking and laughing with his beautiful boy by his side.

"Oh, hey, guys, the weather's coming on. Does that TV work?" Hudson asked, pointing to a small TV lodged awkwardly at the top of the bar.

"Yeah, I think so," I said. I walked behind the bar, grabbed the remote and flicked it on. "What channel?"

"Nine please," his voice rang out excitedly. Way too excitedly for a weather update.

"Oh, that's right," Stirling said with a knowing look. "Hudson's crushing on the weather dude."

Right on cue, the weather forecast started and Liam Wright filled the screen. He was cute in a sweet, preppy kind of way. He was dressed...uniquely, wearing a plaid button-up shirt, a bow tie, and the tightest pair of pants known to mankind.

He started off by talking straight at the camera, but when the map showed up behind him, he had to turn. And when he did, the gasp that fell out of Hudson's mouth was pretty darn sweet.

"That ass is amazing." Porter said what everyone in the room was thinking. "Totally fuckable."

Well, maybe not that part.

"Shhh," Hudson grunted, his eyes transfixed by the screen. I let out a low laugh. Normally I was the *shusher*.

The rest of us chuckled but we didn't say anything else, letting Hudson have his moment with the weather guy. He even mouthed his closing catch phrase, Liam *"I'm always right"* Wright in time with him, before the camera turned back to the anchors. It was actually so adorable that I didn't think any of us were going to give the guy shit about it.

Once the forecast was over, Hudson let out a deep exhale. His face was slightly flushed as he looked over at us.

"Well, I think that definitely cements my answer from before, Steel," Porter said as he walked over to our friend. "Hudson is definitely going to be the next Daddy to get a boy."

Hudson tried to open his mouth to object but didn't get the chance.

"And you know..." Porter stepped right up to Hudson and wagged a finger in front of his face. "I'm always right."

I let out a smile as I pulled my boy in even closer, planting a firm kiss into his forehead. I felt like the luckiest man alive. I was surrounded by friends, I had found a way to use my trust fund for good and best of all, I had someone in my life to share it all with.

Not just someone, though, Nick Macklin.

The most uniquely indescribable boy in the world. No one had ever made me feel the way he did, no one had even come close. He was fearless. Beautiful. Unfiltered. Raw. Honest. Vulnerable. Strong.

"What was that kiss for?" he asked.

I held him tighter, not wanting to ever let him go.

"Nothing." I grinned. "I just...love you."

He turned to me, his brown eyes sparkling oh so naughtily. "Good thing I happen to love you too, then. Right?" His hand landed in the small of my back, before he traced it down...down...and onto my ass.

"I may not be the local weatherman and yes, technically I am stealing his catchphrase," Nick whispered cheekily. "But I'm always right too."

A blissful heat filled my chest. "You are, baby. You are one hundred percent right...for me."

Nick nudged even closer to me, his lips lifting at the edge. "Deffers."

THE END

ABOUT CASEY COX

Contemporary/New Adult MM Romance Author

Casey Cox is devoted to delighting readers with sassy, sweet and sometimes steamy MM gay romance tales of gorgeous, good-hearted and complex men chasing that thing we all love: a guaranteed HEA.

Casey lives on the east coast of Australia, loves the beach and is a proud fur-parent to two utterly adorable, perfectly-perfect French Bulldogs named Ralphie and Lilly.

For more information, please visit
www.caseycoxbooks.com

www.ingramcontent.com/pod-product-compliance
Lightning Source LLC
Chambersburg PA
CBHW061522020726
47502CB00006B/2190